LOVE IN A SNOWSTORM

A PINE HARBOUR NOVEL

ZOE YORK

WWW.ZOEYORK.COM

ISBN: 978-1-989703-49-6
Large print edition, 2021

First printing, 2014

PROLOGUE

Five years earlier

Nothing said unnecessary risk exposure like a man nearing his thirties wading into a teenage house party.

"You need to lighten up, man."

Jake Foster gave his brother Matt a scathing glare. If one of them needed to do anything, it was Matt, and the thing was grow up. "Let's just get Sean and drag him home before the Colonel gets wind of him getting blitzed again."

“Dad needs to lighten up, too.”

“Maybe I should call Dean and get him to shut this party down.” Their older brother was an OPP officer. He wasn’t quite the stick-in-the-mud that Jake had prematurely become, but the two of them were the more responsible pair of brothers by far. Matt and Sean, four and eight years younger respectively, were unapologetic party animals.

They sat in the cab of Jake’s truck, staring at each other for a minute in a futile game of chicken. Jake wasn’t going to call the cops and Matt wasn’t going to push further. Neither of them was happy about having to pick up their drunk-ass brother on a Saturday night.

“Come on, let’s get this over with.” Jake hopped out of the truck and strode up the long country drive of the oversized farmhouse, heading toward the sights and sounds of a party falling apart. Intoxicated, belligerent young people spilled out on the veranda and across the lawn. None of them looked like high school students—mostly college-aged kids. And it sounded like the party had definitely gone awry. Bitter noises filled the air around him about stolen money and not enough beer. He scanned the faces, many of them familiar to him, and a sick feeling filled his gut. Halfway up the drive, he turned around and shoved Matt hard in the chest. “We’re not just picking up Sean, are we? Is Dani in there?”

Matt winced, caught in his half-truth. “She’s the one that called, not Sean. They’re hanging out back where it’s quieter.”

Jake swore under his breath and took off at a run, swerving around two former football players shoving each other. Idiots.

The din faded as they hit the backyard. A smaller group of people sat in a circle, passing a bottle around. One guy had his guitar out. Jake’s heart pounded as he scanned for her face.

"Over here." Her voice lifted into the air behind him and he spun around. They sat on the porch, Sean leaning heavily against her shoulder. She had a hoodie draped awkwardly over half her body, but underneath she was wearing a tiny tank top. He was sure that when she stood up there'd be a few inches of bare skin between her shirt and her snug-as-fuck blue jeans she always wore, and then he'd be screwed.

At least it was dark. There was a passing chance no one would notice that he was turned on by his best friend's little sister.

"Dani, what the hell are you doing here?"

She made a face. "Spare me the lecture, Jake. I came with Sean. Would you rather he be here alone?"

"I'd rather you both be at home watching Saturday Night Live."

"It's the last weekend of the summer. We're all heading back to college and university. Give us a break."

Jake tightened his voice. It was better than growling. "I'll give you a break when you start acting like—"

Matt got between them and held up his hands. "You guys can continue this in the truck." He turned to Sean who gave him a lazy finger and fell backwards. "Come on, bro."

Dani helped push Sean up, but once upright he ambled along with Matt under his own steam. Jake held back, knowing that if he followed too closely he'd end up yelling at Dani again.

Dani Minelli. Rafe's little sister. The only girl between two families of boys. They were all protective of her—except Sean, her accomplice in crime, apparently—and the thought of her getting hurt because of a foolish decision to be reckless made Jake see red.

She stalked ahead, her long, slim denim-clad legs disappearing into the ink black night. If only the rest of her didn't stand out like a beacon for his dick. That tight, white tank top stopped at the tight nip of her waist, and what felt like acres of creamy skin glowed at him above the hip-hugging jeans. Those hips. They were his undoing.

Dani was tall and lanky, but sometime after her seventeenth birthday she'd grown these hips that were meant for holding on to, and Jake had lost his mind. He didn't understand how his brothers kept seeing her as a little sister. The truth was, Jake had never really seen her like that. But she'd been little Dani until all of a sudden she could look him in the eye and when she turned around, he wanted to fall to his knees.

Three years hadn't changed that. Punishing workouts, cold showers, and dating women his own age hadn't changed that. Going to communion hadn't fucking changed that, and the priest hadn't understood what Jake was so worked up over, and suggested he talk to Dani. *Talk to her*. And freak her out for life. Yeah, that wasn't going to happen.

No, Jake planned to take his obsession with Dani Minelli's ass to the grave.

Particularly after his meeting with Mike Fenich earlier that afternoon.

"Jake, my boy," Mike said in his booming voice. "How's your line of credit?"

Since Jake had no social life and an excellent job as one of Mike's foremen with Fenich & Sons Construction, it was pretty good.

"I'm thinking it's time to retire. Gloria wants to go to Florida this winter, and the new cottages we've built will keep me plenty busy in the summer."

Jake's pulse picked up. He'd hoped this conversation might happen one day, but Mike was still young and healthy. Jake mentally did some math. He'd probably be able to swing buying his boss out. And Foster Construction would be more than just a wish and a prayer. It was everything he'd worked for. Everything he'd wanted.

But now as he walked down the drive behind Dani, his hungry gaze devouring that which he could never have, his earlier joy turned bitter on his tongue. He could feel Mike Fenich clapping him on the shoulder. "We'll make this happen before Christmas, Jake. I'm sad I don't have any boys of my own to pass the torch to, but you're not like the rest of the young bucks out there. You keep your nose clean and you work hard. Keep that up and this'll happen, mark my words."

He was twenty-eight to her twenty years. She had three older brothers who would beat the living daylights out of him if he touched her, and Mike Fenich would never let him take over his trusted customers if he started a scandal that would appall the entire population of Pine Harbour—all six hundred gentle souls.

One thing was crystal clear as she hopped onto the running board and leaned into the backseat of his truck. He needed to get over Dani Minelli. And if he managed that feat, he'd buy himself a lottery ticket.

THEY DROPPED off Matt and Sean first, because the Foster family home was closer to the outskirts of town. Jake muttered something to Matt about dumping Sean in the shower and then pulled away from the curb as soon as Matt slammed the door shut behind them. Dani shrank back into her seat. Jake wouldn't even look at her, hadn't continued to yell at her after the aborted lecture at Trudy Sorenson's house.

Pine Harbour was small, and Dani's parents' house was only three blocks into town from the Foster place. Even if she'd wanted to talk to him, there wasn't time.

And she didn't want to talk. She wanted to climb into his pants and down his throat, grab his hands and shove them up her top. She wanted to do all sorts of sweaty, awesome things with Jake, most of which she only had academic knowledge of, but there wasn't a chance in hell he'd be open to any of *that*.

Jake Foster was the most beautiful human being she'd ever laid eyes on. Tall, broad-shouldered and lean-waisted, with legs that went on forever and stretched out a faded pair of jeans or his camp-green Army uniform in all the right places. *All* the right places. Okay, so that wasn't his leg that she imagined behind his fly.

God, she was so immature. She could just imagine how that conversation would go down.

"Jake, I really want to know what your penis looks like. In my imagination it's the most beautiful erection in the world."

"Ew, ick, Dani. By the way, how many erections have you seen? Because Rafe and I have to kill some guys now."

The good news was there would be no murdering, because she hadn't seen any male anatomy up close and in real life. And she was scared to click on most of the Internet links she'd found, so her knowledge was limited to health class text books, Wikipedia and Google Image searches. Which still gave her a lot of comparative data, and left her quite certain that Jake would win the prize for best erection ever.

The thought actually made her mouth water, and that made her blush. She knew people did that—had seen shadows moving at parties and heard more than enough when her brothers thought she wasn't listening. But while she liked kissing and touching—she *really* like touching—she wasn't in a hurry to take the next step. Sex with anyone else sounded messy and raw. Revealing and dangerous.

Sex with Jake would be magical.

Even as she let herself indulge in her favourite fantasy, Dani knew it was ridiculous. Jake was just like any other man. Sex would be sex, nothing more, and she needed to stop pretending otherwise.

And then after the sex, if she was so lucky that Jake would see her as anything other than an over-sized brat, a lifetime of embarrassment would follow. He'd have seen her, all of her, in the basest of ways. And they would grow old with that dirtiest of secrets between them. Yeah, that was a non-starter.

Her entire block was dark and Jake pulled to a silent stop a few houses back. "Your parents don't need to see my headlights in their driveway at this time of night."

It was only midnight and she was an adult without a curfew, but she wasn't going to pick another fight. "Thank you."

He needed to get out to let her out, unless she climbed into the front seat and went out the passenger side. He didn't move. Neither did she. He stared straight ahead and started talking instead, his voice quiet in the even quieter night. "You're a good friend to Sean."

"He's not in trouble. He's just…the baby of the family." She knew all about that. "And no offence, Jake, but I get the impression that you never really had a wild youth."

He laughed, a gentle rumble. "That's probably true." She could see his profile clearly in the moonlight. His jaw was set, his lips straight, and he held that position for what felt like an eternity before he turned to look at her. His face was now almost completely in shadow, and she was suddenly aware that hers would be lit up in comparison. She swallowed hard. *Try not to look like a lovesick fool, Dani*.

"How about you? You're not getting into trouble?"

She shook her head. "I'm pretty head-down, focusing on school."

"Matt said that it looks good for you to do a field placement in Wiarton." Jake's brother was a new-hire paramedic based at the regional hospital thirty minutes south of Pine Harbour. If all went well, she'd be able to get hired on there as a casual paramedic as well. "I don't need to tell you that shenanigans can come back to bite you in the ass later on."

"Shenanigans?" She couldn't hold back a laugh. "I think you're confusing me with your brothers."

"Not possible," his voice rolled toward her from the shadows, sending shivers down her spine. He took a deep breath and turned away, opening his door. "Come on, Cinderella."

She rolled her eyes at him as she climbed out but he just waved her off. She returned the wave, intending it to be the final goodnight, but he fell into step beside her. "Jake, I don't need a walk home." She pointed at the quiet street. "No boogymen, see?"

"Humour me," he said gruffly.

"So how about you, not getting into trouble?" she parroted his earlier question back at him and he gave her a thoughtful look.

"Actually..." He launched into an unexpected share, telling her about an offer Mike Fenich had just made him. It sounded absolutely perfect, actually, and her heart ached at the thought of Jake owning his own business. Not because she didn't want that for him—he'd be an upstanding community leader and an excellent employer, she had no doubt—but it just underlined how far apart their lives were. How insurmountable their age difference. Probably before she came home from college next year he'd be married to a future soccer mom.

"That's wonderful," she whispered, not trusting her voice to hold. They'd reached her house now, and she didn't want him to stop talking.

This was the longest private conversation she'd ever had with Jake. He wasn't staring at her with his usual distrust. He wasn't looking at her at all, but he was sharing and it felt wonderful.

"Yeah. It means a shifting of priorities, but it's the right thing to do."

She caught a sad note as he spoke and forgot her own melancholy for a minute. "Jake?" He blinked and glanced at her briefly before drifting away again, as if he'd forgotten who he was talking to for a minute. "You want to sit?"

He lowered himself to sit on the front steps and braced his feet wide on the flagstone path. He leaned his elbows on his knees and stared across the street. She was used to feeling invisible around him, but it was sort of rude that he never made eye contact. She took a seat next to him, letting herself be close enough that she could feel the brush of his t-shirt against her bare arm. He smelled like spice and man, almost mythic—more fantasy than reality.

“You’re going to be really good at it. Being the boss and all that. You’re so…responsible.” That sounded vaguely insulting. “I mean that in a good way.”

He huffed a small laugh. “I know.”

“Is it scary? Buying a company?”

“A bit. A good kind of scary. It’s motivating. Even if it’s not as glamorous as other jobs.”

She got it. Her parents had both started their own businesses. There was something magical about the unlimited potential of being your own boss. “Don’t sell yourself short. Responsibility is sexy.”

The hot summer night got hotter and the air stopped moving around them. Dani’s face turned red and she wanted the porch to collapse beneath them, or at a minimum for Jake to not have heard her say *that*. Why couldn’t she have used any other word? Good.

Nice. Even attractive wouldn't have made her feel so *juvenile* in comparison to the now painfully uncomfortable *man* next to her. "I didn't…I mean…"

"Goodnight, Dani." His voice was strained as he pushed up and away from the porch. Without thinking, she leapt up and grabbed his forearm, trying desperately not to think about how absolutely awesome it felt under her hand. Hot, silky skin covered in soft, golden hair. Corded muscles flexing as he stood there, still not looking at her. "You should go to bed."

"I'm not a kid." She swallowed hard and stood her ground. "I don't get it. You drive me home, but you can't even stand to look at me. I can't pay you a compliment without you getting weird. All because you see me as Rafe's twelve-year-old kid sister. Newsflash, buddy—I'm a woman."

He turned so slowly that she half expected him to stop long before he did. But he didn't freeze when his gaze connected with hers, or when his upper body had twisted back in her direction. He didn't stop until he turned all the way around and they somehow went from her holding his arm to him holding both of hers. His large, strong hands slid up to firmly grasp her upper arms and he pulled her close.

"I know you're a woman," he said, his words strained. "That's the problem."

"You know…" Suddenly aware of her breathing, Dani tried to play it cool. "You don't see me as a twelve-year-old?"

He gave her a baleful look that revealed just enough masculine hunger to keep her from feeling silly. "No."

Dani had read enough romance novels to know what came next. Her heart pounded in her chest as she stared into Jake's eyes. He was looking at her, really looking at her, and unless she was pathetically mistaken, he wanted to kiss her. Any second now, he'd close the gap between their bodies and she'd feel him hard against her belly. The thought made her weak at the knees and wet between her legs.

But he didn't pull her closer. He didn't move away, either, just held her there, staring. She said his name, quietly at first and then repeated it again a little louder, and he cut her off the second time, his voice strained. "I can't. Your brothers…hell, *my* brothers would kick my ass."

"It's none of their business," she whispered, pressing up on her tiptoes. Maybe she could arch her back and trick him into kissing her.

He frowned. "It'll be everyone's business. And that will be the end of *my* business before it even starts."

"Because of one little kiss?"

His brows knitted together. "It wouldn't be—" He let out a harsh exhale and released her arms only to slide his hands into her hair and pull her face toward his. But his kiss landed on her forehead instead of her lips, and Dani's heart cracked. "Go back to college. Forget that your brother's friend is a dirty old man who likes the way your hips look in blue jeans."

He squeezed the nape of her neck gently before stepping back and lifting his hand in an absent wave as he walked backward down the front walk. She pressed her unkissed lips together and watched in disbelief as the object of her long-held affection drifted away.

CHAPTER ONE

Present day

A funeral sucked at the best of times.

These were far from the best of times.

Dani glanced at the empty glass in her hand. She wished she could get drunk like her family and friends, but she'd volunteered to watch Ryan's three-year-old daughter, Maya. It was the least she could do for her co-worker as he buried the mother of his three young children. Dani couldn't even think about it without yet another sob rising in her throat. Maya's older brothers, Gavin and Jack, were curled up on the couch playing video games on hand-held tablets. Their faces were drawn. Blank. Totally done with the day, and the two weeks that had preceded it.

The funeral had taken some time to organize because of the horrific circumstances around Lynn's death. Circumstances that had landed Dani's own brother, Rafe, in the hospital. He was here today, somewhere, with his ex-wife Olivia. Ex- and soon-to-be once again wife, if Rafe had anything to say about it. That made Dani happy, and God knew that she needed something like that to hold on to.

The investigation into the shooting—which had happened at the marijuana grow-op—was ongoing, and everyone knew it would be months before all the details would be revealed. The autopsy on Lynn Howard's body was semi-public information, however. Their entire small town of Pine Harbour now knew that their friend, daughter and neighbour had quietly been living with ALS, Lou Gherig's

Disease, for almost a year. She'd kept it a secret from her husband for reasons she'd taken to the grave. Her recreational drug use and depression hadn't been a secret, though, and the guilt of that weighed on everyone.

Dani slid a watchful look toward Ryan. They'd worked together ever since she joined Bruce County EMS. He'd been her senior for on-the-job training, and they'd clicked enough to regularly be paired together for shifts—and over the last three years, they'd become close friends as well. He wasn't *talkative*, exactly, but she'd never seen him this withdrawn…ever. Not even in the last two weeks. He'd given a short, sad eulogy at the service, but other than the most basic pleasantries, hadn't spoken to anyone all day. He looked exactly like his sons—done.

Maya crawled out from beneath the dining room table, a cookie crumbling in her chubby little hand. The rest of her was slimming out rapidly as she sprouted into a preschooler, but her hands still had the adorable baby dimples that Lynn had loved to kiss so much. Just thinking that made Dani well up again, and she shoved that grief aside. Tomorrow. She could sob all she wanted tomorrow.

One of the choir members swooped by and took the cookie before Dani could intervene—for fuck's sake, her mother was dead, let her eat a goddamn cookie if it distracted her for a few minutes—and then Maya was on the floor, whimpering for her Mama. That was why Dani couldn't cry…it wasn't her turn.

She sat down next to Maya and held out her hand. "Cuddle?"

The burrowed blonde head wobbled negatively.

Dani wracked her brain for something that might distract her enough. "How about a juice box?"

That earned Dani a long pause before a reluctant, tiny noise squeaked up at her.

"Here you go, kiddo." A long pair of muscular legs appeared in front of them, then folded in half as Jake Foster gruffly delivered an apple juice and two fresh cookies on a paper plate.

Of course it was Jake. Because what she needed on top of grief and confusion was a healthy layer of mixed-up unrequited lust shoved in her face. He had a newly grown beard, not his usual look, and she liked it despite herself. It really wasn't cool for him to take his usual handsome looks and make them extra-sexy at a time like this. It was a neatly trimmed, close-cropped scruff of light brown hair tinted with gold highlights and she wanted to run her palm over it and find out if it was rough or silky. She couldn't decide which sounded better.

"Thank you," Maya said solemnly. She tilted her head to the side and watched Jake suspiciously as she took a cookie, as if to say, *are you going to stop me from eating this cookie right here on this floor, giant man?*

He didn't. Instead, he joined them on the floor, stopping short of sprawling flat on his stomach. Instead, he sat like Dani, but it was close enough to a vote of solidarity for the tiny tot. Maya reluctantly righted herself and leaned against Jake's thigh. He stroked her back with one of his big hands, his long, strong fingers splaying wide across her little torso.

They just sat there, the three of them. After a few minutes, Jake passed the plate over, offering Dani the other cookie. She broke it in half and he took his piece, not quite looking at her.

When one of Maya's friends arrived, she sprinted to the front door to give the other girl a hug. For a second, Dani thought Jake might say something. He didn't. Instead he slowly unwound his long limbs and shoved off the ground. She watched him stop at the coolers by the back door, grab a bottle of beer, and disappear onto the back porch.

Ryan had fought his in-laws over hosting the wake at their house. He lived just up the lane from them, but their home was larger. He wanted the kids to be able to escape to their rooms if they needed to, but when Dani and her brother Tom offered to take the kids home if they wanted, whenever they wanted, Ryan gave in.

The Fenich home was gorgeous. Jake had actually helped build it with Mike Fenich, Lynn's father. Dani was reminded again how close Jake was to the entire Fenich family, and how awful this loss must be for him. Two weeks earlier, the day of the shooting, they'd driven Olivia the four-hour drive south to London, where Rafe had been airlifted for surgery. They'd stayed one night, taking shifts with Olivia at the hospital, and once they knew Rafe was stable but not too keen on visitors, they'd left Olivia there and driven home.

That was the first time Dani and Jake had been alone together in a car—or *anywhere* for more than a few minutes—in five years. Under any other circumstances, she might have found that awkward after wanting him for so long. That day they'd been too tired and sad to care. They hadn't talked much until they arrived in Wiarton, where Jake had left his truck at the hospital. But when she parked, he didn't get out. Instead, he stared out the window for a minute before quietly telling her a couple of random stories about Lynn in high school.

And that was it. She'd listened, then he left. She hadn't seen him since, and she'd been looking. Olivia finally told her that he'd gone hunting up north.

Hoping for more of a connection with him was foolish. She needed to let go of her girly crush. And sometimes she succeeded—she'd dated since college, and when she was with someone else, she managed to lock Jake away in a memory box and pretend she didn't know that he used to have a thing for her. *Forget that your brother's friend is a dirty old man who likes the way your hips look in blue jeans*. The problem was that he may have been able to forget her, but Dani had never met anyone who could light her on fire the way Jake had that night.

God, she was pathetic, hanging on to a handful of words that meant nothing. So he'd gotten a hard-on for a pretty coed. That should be a turn-off, if anything. But it hadn't felt dirty, no matter what he said. The way he'd looked at her had felt special. No, it *had* been special, because for all the frogs—and just regular Joes—she'd kissed since, none of them had looked at her like that. Like she was precious beyond measure.

Except he hadn't looked at her like that again, not once in five years. Not when her brother was shot. Not at countless dances and bonfires, community events or holiday parties. He'd had literally hundreds of opportunities to make a move, and he never had. Never would.

More tears threatened to fall, selfish ones this time, and she had no clue where Maya was. She needed to get a grip and shake it off.

She found the toddler asleep on a chair, still holding on to that cookie. She picked her up, made eye contact with Ryan, and pointed to the door. He nodded, and she tapped Tom on the shoulder on her way out.

Her coat was big enough to wrap around them both, and up at Ryan's house, the lights were already on. Inside she found Derna and Mona from the church tidying the kitchen.

She climbed the stairs to Ryan's room and lay the little girl down in the middle of his bed. He'd warned Dani not to put her in her own room, because she'd been having nightmares and was crying out for him in the middle of the night anyway. The boys ended up in there as well, he'd said. Dani stood in the doorway and took in the room. The closet full of Lynn's clothes, her picture on Ryan's side table. Her jewellery box overflowing on the top of her dresser. Dani finally gave in to the tears she'd been fighting all day and sank to her knees, great big silent sobs wracking her shoulders.

Once she pulled herself together and splashed some water on her face, she made a firm resolution. Life wasn't fucking fair, and a stupid crush was such a pathetic problem to have. She was officially done feeling sorry for herself. Jake Foster didn't own a part of her heart any longer. She was a grown woman, looking for a man who wanted to love her. And all of her feelings would be poured in that direction, nowhere else.

Downstairs, she accepted a cup of tea from Mona.

"Still busy down the road, love?" Derna asked, handing over a plate of cookies she didn't need.

Dani took two and nodded.

"You okay here on your own with the little one? We're almost done here. Did some vacuuming.

Stocked the cupboards. It was a good chance to do it. Ryan hasn't wanted any help."

"I'll be fine, thank you. Tom will be along soon with the boys. And one of us will stay overnight if Ryan lets us." Although he wouldn't. And she didn't blame him. His kids didn't need all those sympathetic adult eyes on them as they grieved.

Her brother showed up a few minutes later, and had Gavin and Jack upstairs and brushing their teeth with imaginary chocolate sauce in record time. Tom was a park ranger and a born entertainer.

Ryan followed along within the hour. When he came in, he went straight for the bottle of scotch in the kitchen cupboard.

Dani stood in the doorway. On the one hand, the man had just buried his wife. Fuck it. On the other…he was going to kick them out soon and be the sole caregiver to three young children. All of whom would probably sleep next to him. The paramedic in her couldn't stay silent.

"How many drinks have you had?" She gave him a small smile and sat across the table from him. *No judgement, I promise*. "I don't care if you want to get tanked tonight. But if you do, let me stay, okay? I'll sleep with Maya in her room."

He just stared at her for a minute, but it was more of a stare *through* her. "I didn't have anything earlier," he finally muttered. "This is my one and only drink for the night."

"It would be understandable—"

He laughed, and it was a cold, hard cut-off. "We took the same grief workshops, Dani. We've seen this how many times? I know. I know everything you're going to say. And you know what? None of it matters inside my head right now. This is going to be the only drink I have tonight, but it's sure as fuck not the only one I *want*."

She nodded.

Tom's footsteps sounded on the stairs, then he appeared in the doorway. "Boys are tucked in to their room with a movie on my iPad, but they were asking about crawling in with Maya. I didn't know…"

Ryan sighed and tipped his glass, swirling the amber liquid around. "Yeah, I'll go up in a minute. Thanks for keeping an eye on them today."

"Do you need anything else brought over from the Fenichs' place?" Tom asked.

"Nah."

Dani watched her brother head for the door, but she didn't get up yet. Ryan finished his drink and shoved his glass to the centre of the table.

"Captain says you've asked for an extended leave of absence from work."

He made a noncommittal noise in the back of his throat.

"I don't know what that means."

He glared at the bottle of scotch, then shoved away from the table and stuck it back in the cupboard. "It means that I'm not ready to leave my kids with anyone overnight. Or even during the day. I want to be here to send them off to school and pick them up when they get off the bus."

"I could help."

"No." He barked it out, but she didn't flinch. They'd worked together for almost three years, and been partnered up for most of that. They'd clicked in part because Dani didn't mind Ryan's grouchiness. She'd grown up with three older brothers, two of whom could out-grouch Ryan any day of the week. Tom was the nice one. "I'm not—I can't create a temporary routine for them like that with another woman. No offence."

She offered a rueful smile. None taken. "I get it. I just want to do something to ease your burden."

"Tell everyone to back off. That would help."

"Kay. I'm on shift the next three days, but how about I come over for lunch mid-week? I'll play dolls with Maya and you can take a nap or something."

He swore under his breath and she grinned. "Sure, that sounds good."

"I'm not going to stop worrying about you."

He gave her a ghost of a smile. "You should head back down to the wake. There's a ton of food."

"Conversation's over?"

"For now."

They weren't really huggers, but she gave him an awkward one-armed squeeze anyway.

He walked her to the door and mumbled his thanks. As soon as she stepped onto the deck, he locked the door behind her and turned out the kitchen light.

"He okay?" Jake's voice drifted toward her from the dark and she closed her eyes.

"He will be. What are you doing out here?"

"Tom came back without you. It's dark."

She grumbled something under her breath that she didn't even understand herself, but as she got closer to him she realized it didn't matter. He was drunk. His eyes were bright and his smile was sloppy. That he was smiling at all would have been her first clue. "You shouldn't be stumbling around while intoxicated. It's not safe."

He shrugged and nodded his head down the lane. A car crawled toward them, some of the guests leaving. "Needed some air. You can see me back safely."

A lazy snowflake fell from the sky, landing on her nose. She narrowed her eyes as she fell into step next to him. "I thought that's what you were doing."

"Mutually beneficial something or other." His words had a slight slur to them, but he wasn't stumbling at all. He walked with ease in a relatively straight line. But he was definitely too drunk to drive himself home.

"Come on, let's find your brothers."

"Matt and Sean just left." He yawned. "Dean will be back in a bit. He just drove his girlfriend home."

"The woman from Port Elgin?" That was more than an hour round trip. Dani sighed. "I'll drive you home."

"It's fine. I don't mind staying late and keeping Mike company."

But inside they found the gathering winding down pretty quickly, and both Mike and Gloria Fenich looked like they were ready for bed.

Dani pulled out her phone and texted Dean to find out his ETA.

> **Dean: Prop him up on the porch with a beer. I'll be there in forty-five minutes.**

She couldn't do that. He'd come to find her in the dark. It was the least she could do to see him home safely.

> **Dani: Snow's coming. I'll drive him home.**

She said her goodbyes, then looked for Jake. She winced as she caught sight of him slowly pacing on the porch. The tight, pinchy feeling in her gut that she always got around him had returned. Damnit. *Get over him, get over him, get over him*. She took a deep breath and pushed herself back out into the cold. "Looks like I'm your ride tonight, come on."

He made a face. "Sorry."

"Don't worry about it."

Her car was parked halfway up the lane and the sad absurdity of the situation struck her out of the blue. She laughed to herself.

"What's so funny?"

She tipped her head up to the night sky, letting snowflakes drop on her face. "Oh, nothing." *Second time in two weeks we're alone. I've walked up and down this lane half a dozen times today. The universe has a cruel sense of humour the way it yanks you in and out of my life.* "A bunch of random nonsense. It's been a long day."

She unlocked the car with a click of the button on her keychain and watched as Jake folded himself into her passenger seat before walking around to the driver's side. It took a minute for the car to warm up, but she wasn't going to just sit there, so she gripped the freezing cold steering wheel and headed up to the highway. Well, highway was overstating it. But the two-lane corridor up and down the peninsula was what counted for a major road in the wilds of northern Bruce County.

Ryan lived just south of town. Jake's house was on the north end, around the harbour, into the country that butted back onto the provincial parks. In between lay Pine Harbour, their sleepy little village of six hundred people. Dani still lived at home because who was she kidding about having a social life? All the eligible men in Pine Harbour were either Minellis or Fosters. Half of them were her brothers. The other half were Jake's brothers. And Jake.

Mr. Drunk as a Skunk.

Not really. It would be easier to stay grumpy with him if he didn't bring little girls cookies and come find her in the dark. And sober up far too fast.

"Tough day," he said quietly, staring at her. She peered ahead through the snow, not wanting to look over at him. Except she *totally* wanted to look over at him and find some comfort and company in his chocolate brown eyes.

"Yep."

"Back to work tomorrow?"

She nodded. "I've used up all my available time off." They all had, although Jake owned his own business. He worked hard, and she knew that, but it didn't stop her from lashing out a little bit. Not fair, but he was the closest target and it had been a long, roller coaster kind of day. "You went hunting, eh?"

Out of the corner of her eye, she saw him look away. He didn't answer. She turned into town. Pine Harbour was hidden from the main road by a concession of forest, but on the other side, past Mac's Diner and the gas station, stretched ten square blocks of small town fun. Or terrifying boredom, depending on one's proximity to one's teenage years.

Dani turned right at the main intersection and headed north again, the town fading away as quickly as it appeared. She'd only been to Jake's house twice, but she knew the route by heart. His was the last lane at the end of this road. He'd built his house himself. It was heartbreakingly gorgeous, just like him.

Stone pillars topped with LED lanterns flanked the end of his drive, lighting the snow-drifted entrance to his lane.

Parked right in front of the house was a red Jeep, lights on and engine running.

Dani slowed to a stop behind the other car and glanced over at Jake. She was just giving a friend a ride home after a funeral. She didn't have any right to ask him who the leggy chick getting out of the Jeep was. But she did have a right to want him out of her car, immediately. "Someone who could have picked you up?"

CHAPTER TWO

When Jake told Tasha she should come down on her next weekend off, he hadn't thought she'd take him up on it. He hadn't even told her about the funeral, just said he needed to get back to Pine Harbour for work.

Prickly discomfort crawled up his back as Dani stared at him. He was pretty sure he hadn't done anything wrong, but he was on the ugly side of five beers and a couple of shots of whiskey. "She's a friend from up north. I wasn't expecting her." He popped open the door, because the woman he'd sort of been seeing

—for a single night, and some casual flirtation before that—was standing outside his house. What else could he do? “Do you want to come out and meet her?”

Dani’s eyes flared wide in that familiar, *Jake, you totally don’t get me* look he hated because no, he totally didn’t get her. She shook her head. “It’s snowing. I should get home.”

“Wait.” He waved at Tasha, who looked bundled up enough in a parka and oversized toque to wait a minute, and closed the door again. “Listen. I’m…” *What?* There was no end to that sentence that wouldn’t open a can of worms. “We should have coffee soon.”

Dani shook her head. “It’s been a long, emotional day. Week. Month. But I don’t think that’s a good idea.”

“I’ve been thinking about you a lot lately.”

Her eyes narrowed. “You’re drunk, Jake. And I have to get home.” She nodded in Tasha’s direction—*fuck*—and sighed. "And you have a guest."

"And if I didn't?"

She laughed and looked straight ahead. "That's the douchiest thing I've ever heard come out of your mouth, Jake Foster. Get out of my car."

Shit. He hadn't meant it like however she'd taken it, but he wasn't thinking straight. "I'm going to ask you again when I'm sober."

"Okay." She said like it was anything but. Like if she wasn't as polite as she was, her retort would have been a brusque *"Whatever"*.

He climbed out of her sedan and carefully shut the door. He nodded at Tasha, who slowly approached him. She lifted her hands tentatively, like she wasn't sure if she could hug him. He was painfully aware of Dani's car driving away—that they were visible in her rearview mirror, and he stepped back and gestured to his door. “Hey, Tasha. Come on in.”

Inside he paused for a second, then realized he was being a terrible host. “Can I take your coat?”

She nodded and shrugged out of it. “Is it okay that I stopped by? You said…”

“I know. Yeah, it’s fine. I was just at a funeral.” He looked at her. They’d known each other for almost a year, and when he’d gone up to the hunting lodge she worked at after the shooting, he’d finally taken her up on months of open invitations. *Fuck*. This was a woman he’d slept with, and he was treating her like a stranger. “Hey. It’s nice to see you.” He pulled her in for a hug, then waved his hand around his foyer. “Welcome to my house, I guess. This is a bit of a surprise.”

She rocked back on her heels and tucked her thumbs into the back pockets on her jeans. “Nice place.” She grinned. “I’m heading to

Toronto tomorrow, but I thought you might put me up for the night?"

"Of course." Jake chewed on his lower lip, biting back an offer for her to use his spare room. What the hell was that about? Tasha would have gone ahead to her sister's place in Port Elgin if she just wanted a bed to crash in. She was offering something as much as asking, and no part of him wanted to take her up on it. "Want a coffee?" He needed to sober up. And figure out where his head was at.

"Lead the way." She offered him that same open smile that had sucked him in a week earlier. Man, it was tempting. But it was one thing to have a fling with her in Tobermory. It was another to sleep with her in the house he'd built for Dani. *Fuck, fuck, fuck.* He needed to stop thinking about it like that.

Dani. How fucked up their relationship had become. He'd spent her last year away at college trying to think of a way he could ask her out without causing WWIII with her brothers. He'd poured himself into the design and construction of this house, ostensibly as a way to make a splash with the rebranded Foster Construction, but deep down he'd always thought of it as proof that he was good enough for her. That he could be a serious suitor, even if that was ridiculously old-fashioned.

And then she'd moved home. Four years didn't ease the ache he'd felt when she'd brought a boyfriend with her. The guy didn't actually move to Pine Harbour, but he was around. A lot. Enough that Dani was once again off-limits. Which was Jake's own fault for pushing her away.

He poured water into the coffee maker. He'd been caulking the sink when Rafe stalked into his half-finished house and started ranting about how his sister was spending the night at her boyfriend's place. He'd made a complete mess of the job and didn't bother to fix it until the next day when his hangover faded away.

Not much different than tonight. Except tonight he'd been drinking in memory of a woman who'd been like a sister to him. And she was gone. Dani wasn't gone, but she still felt brutally off-limits…

God, how many missed opportunities had he had? Over the last few years, those opportunities had faded away. She'd grown up, and that possibility he'd always seen in her eyes—that he'd felt like a pervert for wanting to act on—it disappeared. Wariness and judgement took its place as she turned into a grown woman who had no time for a man like him.

Someone who stands still and lets life swirl past him while he thinks too damn hard.

"Jake?" He blinked up at Tasha, who was staring at him with a saucy look on her face. "I don't feel like I've got your full attention."

He made an apologetic face. She wasn't wrong.

"Would this help?" She grabbed the hem of her sweater and peeled it off. Underneath she wore a loose tank top. And under that… nothing. She was beautiful, he couldn't ignore that. His dick perked up, because it had no soul, and when she sauntered around the counter and pressed herself against him, he thought about giving in. It would be easy. And fun. And he didn't have enough of either of those in his life right now.

But he'd have another woman on his mind. He couldn't ignore the disturbing reality that Tasha looked a bit like Dani, too. Tall. Long legs. Dark wavy hair. Pretty. *God, he was a pig.* But only one of them made him want to build a house so they could fill it with babies, and it wasn't the woman in his arms.

He sighed and gave her a friendly hug. "I'm sure that always helps, Tash, but I'm not in the mood tonight."

"Really?" She pulled back and gave him a look of genuine surprise. That made two of them.

He certainly hadn't thought twice about sleeping with her nine days earlier.

He squeezed her hips and eased her a step back. "I hope I didn't give you the wrong impression?"

"No…I'm a big girl." She cocked her head. "Is this about the funeral? Because we can just cuddle. Or I could give you a—"

He cleared his throat. He didn't need her to finish that offer. "It's more that I thought what we had was a one-time only thing."

She arched her eyebrows, like she didn't really believe him. "Then the invitation to visit was a bit silly."

"I meant it at the time. You leave quite an impression on a guy."

She shrugged and nudged her way past him to take over making the coffee he'd stared at for God knows how long. "Okay."

"I'll make up the spare room for you."

She grinned over her shoulder. “That sounds like an unnecessary waste of clean sheets when we could keep each other warm tonight, but whatever.”

Whatever indeed. He beat a quick retreat upstairs before he gave in to the base part of him that appreciated when a beautiful woman wanted into his bed.

“I’M FINE.” Ryan swung his door open, letting Jake step inside.

“Good.”

“Really.”

Jake didn’t bother to respond again. Ryan was obviously *not* fine. He hadn’t shaved in days, and his red-rimmed, dark-shadowed eyes suggested he may not have slept much in the same period of time.

A week had passed since the funeral. They'd slipped into the beginning of December, and life kept swirling on. Jake knew from his older brother, Dean, who'd been one of the OPP officers on the scene at the grow-op bust when Lynn was shot, that the investigation was still ongoing.

Three police officers had been shot as well, and one of them—a tactical officer from elsewhere in the province—hadn't made it. The other two, Rafe Minelli and Trent Bradford, would make full recoveries, but they were local boys. Dean and Rafe and Ryan were all good friends. They'd all grown up with Lynn. There was no corner of Pine Harbour that this tragedy didn't reach.

Jake held up the yearbooks he'd dug out of his father's attic. "I thought you might want to see these. Lynn practically wrote a novel in mine our graduating year."

That wasn't exactly the real reason for his visit, but it made a good excuse. While Dean had called Ryan a couple of times, and seen him at the funeral, he hadn't been out to visit yet. And this morning over breakfast at Mac's, Dean had asked Jake to check in on Ryan.

Go yourself, asshole, Jake had said, slapping the diner table between them. Dean had shifted uncomfortably in his seat. *Fuck*, Jake had thought. He got it. Dean had been on the scene, and he hadn't ended up shot. Somehow it was different for Rafe, who'd tried to save Lynn's life. They all knew that Dean had just been doing his job. Lynn had been shot by one of the growers, not a cop. But guilt didn't always understand logic. *Shit like this tears friendships apart*. And Jake knew too much about letting friendships slip through his fingers because of stupidity and silence. So here he was, his brother's messenger boy. "We're all worried about you."

"We're surviving." Ryan pointed to a steaming pot of coffee. "Just put some on, you want?"

"Sure. Kids are at school?"

"Boys are. Maya's upstairs having a nap."

Jake nodded.

"The boys will like the yearbooks," Ryan added as he filled two mugs. He stared at the carafe for a second as he shoved it back into the machine, his lips pulled thin. "I mean, I will too."

Jesus. Jake didn't know what to say. *It's okay if you're pissed off at your wife for getting killed?* It was okay, but it didn't sound okay. "Milk in the fridge?"

"Yeah." Ryan grabbed an almost empty sugar bowl from the counter and two spoons while Jake got the milk. Busy work instead of awkward-as-fuck conversation. Fair enough. Jake fixed his cup as he liked it, then passed the milk jug to his friend. Ryan waved it away and sighed. "I'm not the greatest company."

"That's grief, man. It's selfish. Gotta be. Only way to give yourself space inside to deal."

"People keep saying that." Ryan twisted his spoon in his cup.

"It's true."

Ryan blinked slowly a few times before responding. "You lost your mother, right?" His words came out in a rough, scratchy rush.

Jake nodded. "I was ten. Sean was just a toddler. Dean was twelve and Matt was five." Ryan hadn't moved to Pine Harbour until he married Lynn, so he only knew the Colonel as a gruff older man—a retired officer who showed up to regimental Christmas dinners. "It was hard on my father. You're doing okay." Jake respected his father, but it hadn't been easy. For any of them.

They sat and drank coffee in silence for a few minutes. Ryan was the first to break it, with a sigh. "Their teacher sent a note home yesterday reminding me to send apple sauce."

Jake didn't really follow, and his confusion must have been obvious on his face.

"I'm all they have now and I don't even know what Gavin and Jack take in their lunch."

"You need to send apple sauce? What kind of fucked up school rule is that?"

Ryan shook his head. "No. But Gavin loves it. And I didn't know."

"He didn't tell you?"

The corners of Ryan's mouth tugged down. "He's not talking a lot right now." He tipped his chair back, rocking on the back legs. "God, I just want the world to pause for a minute. Just long enough for my kids to figure out that I'm not going anywhere."

Jake remembered that ache, that everyone around him was happy about birthday parties and Christmas, and he just wanted his mom back. He could still taste that strange bitter resentment in the back of his throat, even after twenty-two years. "I'm sorry, man."

Ryan closed his eyes and shrugged.

"Something specific going on?"

"Lynn's sister is coming up for a family dinner next weekend. Gloria came by after the boys caught the bus this morning to give me the heads up. Apparently she's engaged."

Jake froze, his pulse thudding like sludge in his veins. "Oh?" Rafe was going to propose to Olivia soon. *Shit like this tears apart friendships.* "That must have been hard to hear."

"Never mind. File that under the grief being selfish thing."

"Okay."

"I can't help it. I don't want to see anyone be fucking happy right now. Her sister just died. Her niece and nephews lost their mom, and she's going to be…." Ryan rubbed a hand over his lower face and grunted. "It doesn't matter. I can keep it inside."

From upstairs, Maya cried out, and Ryan shoved to his feet.

"Do you want me to head out?"

"Nah. It's time for her to get up, and she'll be happy to see someone other than me. She's got a new My Little Pony she'll be thrilled to tell you all about."

While Ryan went to get his daughter, Jake pulled out his phone and tapped a quick message to Dean. Next, he called his foreman overseeing the final days of interior work on a new build house they'd sold. "Hey Johnny, did the tiler finish up?"

The sounds of a busy construction site filled his ear. "Yeah, but I haven't seen the plumber yet. Can you text me his number?"

That's what Jake liked about his foreman. He didn't ask if Jake could call the guy. He'd do it himself. Jake would bump up his Christmas bonus for that little gesture. "Sure thing."

When he hung up, he realized he didn't have the number in his phone—or couldn't find it, which was more likely. Every time the damn thing had an update, everything changed. He kept a paper backup of everything in his truck, so he threw his coat on and jogged outside.

Right into Dani.

He skidded to an awkward stop. “Hey. Hi.”

“Jake.” She said his name with wariness, which didn’t surprise him. She hadn’t responded to his text thanking her for the ride home after the wake. And he couldn’t get the memory of her calling him a douche out of his head, but while he’d picked up the phone a few times, he hadn’t been convinced she’d want to hear from him, and had aborted each call before connecting.

“I sent you—” he said at the same as she started, “I got your message, I just…”

They shared a nervous laugh, then he pointed around her to his truck. “I need to get something…for work. But then I’m heading back inside. I’m having a cup of coffee with Ryan, and Maya just woke up.”

"Perfect timing." She held up a small cooler bag. "I brought tiny sandwiches and cookies to have a tea party with her."

He couldn't keep the smirk off his face. Even as his lips twitched, he knew she was going to take him to town.

"What? You're not scared of playing make believe with a little girl, are you?" She didn't hide the scorn in her voice.

"Course not. But Maya and I already have plans to look at a My Little Pony."

"Ahhh." She stepped past him. "I'll just have to invite Rainbow Dash to join us."

He turned and watched her stomp into the house, her long brown hair swinging loose down her back. Yeah, he definitely should have called her.

He stayed outside on his phone for almost twenty minutes, despite the cold. Work stuff didn't take long, but Dani had knocked him off-kilter, as she always did. So after he responded to a few work emails, he surfed the net for a few minutes, being a coward. By the time he went back in, the tea party was almost over. Three year olds apparently moved at the speed of light when excited.

He finished his coffee, but the earlier conversation with Ryan wasn't going to resume. And with the frosty reception Dani was giving him, he knew it would be best to cut his losses. He was surprised Dani stood up when he announced he was heading out.

"I'm going to head out as well," she said, dusting off her knees from sitting on the floor. He had to force himself not to stare at her. As always, he was torn between not wanting to reveal how much he wanted her and needing to hungrily soak up every bit of her that he could—the inviting crease of her jeans at her hips, the way her soft black sweater curved over her breasts and showed a hint of shadow where her necklace dropped into the V-neck.

"You can stay," he said lamely, feeling stupid when she rolled her eyes.

"I could," she retorted drily. "Thanks for the permission."

He lifted both hands to say, *my bad*, and said goodbye to both Ryan and Maya. Once outside, he stood on the porch for a minute, replaying the conversations—the night of the funeral, and when she arrived today. Where could he have turned it around? What could he have said differently? He hesitated there, and before he could depart, Dani stepped outside and joined him.

"I owe you an apology," he said in a hurry. Might as well get it over with.

"No, you don't," she muttered, heading down the stairs toward her car.

He followed her. "Listen…" he trailed off, but damn it, they needed to clear the air. "I wasn't hitting on you."

She lifted her brows, giving him a bland, disinterested look. “Pardon?”

“Cut it out, Dani. You know what I’m talking about.” *Shut up*, said a small voice inside him. *This isn’t the way to go*. He ignored it.

“I haven’t the foggiest.”

“When I suggested we have coffee. That wasn’t a come-on.” All the ways he’d imagined confessing how much he wanted her, telling her over coffee wasn’t even on the list.

“You asked me if I’d have a different answer if you hadn’t had a girl waiting for you. Don’t forget that part.” She stopped beside his truck as if to say, *you stop here. Don’t follow me to my car*. She was smart to do that, because he would have. Now that they were talking, they weren’t stopping, even if they were standing on Ryan’s lawn.

He took a deep breath and exhaled slowly. “She’s a friend. You could have come inside.”

"So you haven't slept with her?" She finally met his gaze and the fire in her eyes almost knocked him over.

Damnit. This was not how the conversation was supposed to go. "I didn't sleep with her that night."

"Oh, gross."

"That's mature," he snarled. As soon as he said it, he hissed, wanting to take it back, but it was too late.

CHAPTER THREE

They were this close to having a knock-down, drag-out fight over a nothing conversation. *Not the conversation. The woman*. She hated seeing Jake with others. He didn't date a lot, but when he did it was like a hot blade slicing right through her middle. "I didn't say it was gross because it involved sex, you Neanderthal! I just don't need any details about you screwing another woman."

That admission strung out between them like a fragile bubble, all shiny and wobbly in the wind. Attention grabbing in a *don't touch it or it'll pop* kind of way. He glowered at her, and for a minute she was sure he'd move away from it. Now wasn't the time. It was never the time. If there'd ever *been* a time, it would have been the night of the wake, but he'd had a *friend* visiting him.

"Why is that?" His voice dropped to a low, smoky note that made her quiver from the inside out, and she wanted to punch him for affecting her.

"You know why." Of that she was now sure. He knew, and he didn't do anything about it.

He shook his head, stepping back. Right on schedule. "I just wanted to apologize. When I asked you… Given all that's gone on, I really just wanted to reconnect with you."

The bald-face lie burned at her. For five long years, she'd settled into the narrative that he didn't want her. But the way he was looking at her now? There wasn't anything *friendly* about it. She wasn't going to hide how she felt. Maybe putting it out there and being rejected again was the only way to finally move forward. “There’s only one way I want to reconnect with you, Jake, and it’s not as friends over coffee.” She’d barely spit the words out, an angry, hurt mess of feelings, before the house door swung open behind Jake.

Ryan and Maya stepped outside, and Jake took a giant step back, staring at the ground.

“Dannnniiiii!” The blond tornado tumbled down the stairs and across the snowy lawn toward them, launching herself against Dani’s legs. “You no go home!”

“Jake and I were just talking for a minute.” She crouched for one last kiss. “I’m going now. Where are you going?”

“Get my bwothers from the bus!”

“Cool, you have fun.” Dani stood and waved at Ryan, then waited until the father and daughter duo were safely out of earshot before turning her attention back to Jake. She walked around him, giving him a wide berth as she headed for her car.

But she wasn't leaving without calling him on his shit. *In for a penny…* "You know what? You need to dissuade yourself of this misguided idea that I'm somehow an innocent young girl that you're not allowed to be attracted to. We are equals. We are both *adults*. And as an adult woman, I'm telling you to get your head out of your ass."

"Even if I wanted to—"

Dani snapped. This wasn't the first time they'd had this conversation, although that night five years earlier had been…sweet. This wasn't sweet. This was raw and bitter and laced with regret. "You *do* want to. Need I remind you that—"

"This isn't the time, Dani." He was practically yelling now, so unlike him. She liked getting under his skin, making him mad. This was good.

So she pushed a little harder. “It’s been five years. I’m guessing there’s never been a good time.”

He raked his hand back through his hair, his jaw set firmly and his eyes glittering with no longer disguised frustration. “Ryan wants the world to stop spinning. His sister-in-law just got engaged.”

Dani reeled backwards, emotionally and literally. She felt unsteady on her feet for more than one reason. “That’s…kind of shitty. But I don’t see what it has to do with us.”

“Rafe and Olivia…” Jake trailed off, an unhappy look ghosting across his face before he scowled again. “And they make sense. You and me…we’re like matches and a jug of kerosene.”

Yeah. Now she got the picture. Once again, the chemistry between them was taking a backseat to everything else. And this time, she couldn’t argue with him, because he was putting Ryan first.

"It's almost Christmas, Dani. Everyone is fucking happy and he's barely holding it together." He stepped closer, but not close enough. Not reassuringly close. "I can't deny that I want you." God, that was a bittersweet admission after all this time. "But now's really not the time. But I'm hoping we can…be friends. For now."

"You know what? It's okay. The fact that we've danced around each other for so long and never acted on it…it's probably a sign." She lifted her hands in the air, as if it was just that easy. *If only*. "I'm done."

"Done what?" He shifted again, and suddenly he loomed over her, stealing her breath. "You've never given us a chance, either. I'm just asking for some time."

"You just finished telling me that there is no *us*. So time…sure, take all the time you need." She pressed herself to the full extent of her height. He was less than half a foot taller than her, but he was broad. And fierce.

She might be able to do fiery and pissed off, but he was a caged tiger. Staring him down wasn't easy.

Mostly because this close, with this much emotion stewing between them, she just wanted to kiss him.

But it wasn't *the time*. Fuck him. He could take all the time he wanted. She wasn't waiting.

She was moving on.

THREE LONG, scowl-filled weeks passed without seeing Jake again. The usual round of holiday parties were canceled or limited to family only. As close as the Fosters and Minellis were, they didn't have any combined celebrations this year. Even Rafe and Olivia's second wedding was shaping up to be family only, just a private dinner on New Year's Eve at a restaurant for their siblings and parents.

Dani was glad she wasn't going to spend their marriage celebration ignoring Jake. That would be awkward.

She was hiding in her bedroom mid-afternoon on Christmas Eve—the least festive, most somber holiday in her memory—wishing that she'd volunteered to work the day shift. She'd be heading in to work after an early dinner, but frankly, she could have done a 24-hour shift. Her black mood was best suited to being behind the wheel of an ambulance, not playing dutiful daughter and sister.

Someone knocked tentatively on her door.

"Come in," she called out.

Her once and soon-to-be-again sister-in-law, Olivia, slowly pushed the door open and stepped inside. "You don't sound like you really want company."

"Meh. I like you."

"Can I hide in here for a bit?"

"Sure."

"You've been scarce the last few weeks."

Dani shrugged. "I've been working a lot. Visiting with Ryan and kids when I'm not."

"Rafe has been there a few times. It sounds like they're doing okay."

"Yeah." Dani looked down at her flannel sleep pants and t-shirt. "I should get dressed now that people are arriving, eh?"

"It's just your brothers." Olivia giggled as Dani shot her a look of mock horror. "I know, I won't say that in front of your mother."

Anne Minelli liked things to be done a certain way, including—especially—family meals. They didn't have a lot of those after Rafe and Olivia had broken up. And this was the first year in a few that Zander would be home for a full week. Her oldest brother was in the Army, a full-time soldier stationed out West. He'd fly back on New Year's Day, after the intimate wedding.

"Hey, I had a meeting with Jake a couple of days ago about some construction work we need done for the movie"—Olivia was the on-site lackey for a film production coming to Pine Harbour in the spring— "and…he was grumpy. I'm not used to that from him. It's more of a Minelli trait."

Dani glowered at her for real this time.

"Exactly. Just like that." Olivia winked. "And his mood got even worse when I innocently mentioned you—"

"Oh God, why did you do that?"

"Couldn't help myself." Her friend shrugged. "What's going on?"

Dani sighed and threw herself back on the bed. "It's a long story."

"Excellent. I'm in no hurry to go downstairs."

So Dani filled her in, trying to be objective on all points. She might have failed when it came to describing dropping Jake off at his house for a booty call. And she definitely kept some of the hotter details to herself, like the intense way Jake stared at her mouth or what it felt like to have his hands on her. She hadn't forgotten in five years. She feared she never would.

Olivia listened to the recounting of the last fight with her hand over her mouth, her eyes wide. "Wow."

"What?"

She shook her head. "Jake's being a real jerk."

"No, he's…" Yeah, he was totally being a jerk. "Is it bad that I want to defend him? He didn't see this coming."

"Yes, that's awful. Don't excuse him. That's how five years of silent crushing has slipped by."

"Damnit."

"You need to show him that you won't wait for him to screw his head on straight."

She'd already made that decision. "I told him as much."

Olivia leaned in. "You need to *show* him."

"Is that what you did to win back my brother?" Dani waved her hand in the air. "No, don't tell me. I don't want to know."

"Rafe and I didn't talk enough. It sounds like you and Jake talked too much. Not well, not calmly…"

Dani nodded miserably. That was exactly the problem. "Maybe we're just not meant to be." That physically hurt her to say out loud, even though she'd said as much to Jake a few weeks earlier.

"Is there any doubt about how you feel about him?"

"No." And didn't that just make her feel helpless?

Olivia softened her voice. "And do you know that he wants you, too?"

"Yes."

"So boy likes girl, and vice versa. But that knowledge isn't moving you guys forward. What you need to do is show him what he's got to lose." Olivia got a positively evil gleam in her eye. "Make him jealous."

Dani thought about all that had come out since she'd seen that woman at Jake's house the night of the wake. Jealousy certainly had spurred a lot of feelings to be dumped on the table.

It was evil. It wasn't mature or responsible. And fuck it all, she was game. "I wouldn't even know where to start."

Olivia rolled her eyes. "Oh, come on. He loses his mind every time you have a boyfriend. All you have to do is hug another man and he'll drag you to the nearest dark corner."

Dani just blinked at her friend. Really? She'd never seen any evidence of that. "And you see that, but Rafe has no clue?"

"I think that's a case of willful blindness. On the part of all of your brothers. And Jake's, too."

"And you've never talked to Rafe about this?"

Olivia laughed. "No. That would put my own sex life in peril, and I just got it back." She sighed. "You'll tell your brothers when you're good and ready."

"There's nothing to tell."

"Not yet. But there will be one day."

Your lips to God's ears. But it certainly didn't feel likely from where Dani stood.

Dinner was quiet, but drama-free, and everyone else headed out for the Christmas Eve Mass at the same time she left for work.

Since Ryan was off on leave, every shift had her partnered with a random paramedic—filling vacation holes, basically. Tonight it was all younger EMS workers on shift, and Matt Foster was waiting for her in the staff lounge with a smirk on his face. He lazily tossed his feet on the chair opposite and stretched his big, muscular body in all directions. “You drew the short stick tonight, Minelli.”

“Aw…afraid I’ll put you to shame from the driver’s seat?” As the junior paramedic in a new pairing, she knew she’d be expected to drive the bus and she didn’t mind at all.

“Tell you what. You do the rig check in under forty-five minutes, and I’ll drive tonight.”

She blew a raspberry. “We both know that’s not a good idea.”

“Don’t think you can do it?”

“Oh, I know I can do it.”

“Fine. Sub-forty-five check, and I’ll buy your drinks on our next night off together. You blow it, and the tab’s on you.”

She leaned over the chair his feet were propped on and gave him an innocent look. “Don’t count your beer steins before they’re filled." Yanking the chair back, she shoved it under the table as his legs hit the floor. "Come on, you can time me."

"I was going to finish my coffee!"

"I can time myself…"

"Fat chance. I'm coming."

Forty-three minutes later, she triumphantly shoved a completed checklist in his face.

"Good job." He braced his arm on the side of the ambulance and grinned at her. "You off on the 27th?"

"Yep."

"The Green Hedgehog. It's a date."

The collegial acceptance meant a lot to her, and if she was smart, she'd leave it at that. But his words reverberated through her head. Who would make Jake more jealous than his handsome, out-going, younger brother? She couldn't tell him, but Matt was a total player. He wouldn't be offended if she flirted with him a bit. Probably wouldn't even notice.

"Excellent, I'm looking forward to drinking all of your beer. You'll drive?"

He laughed. "Sure thing, baby girl."

Okay, so maybe it would be a *little* challenge to get him to flirt with her.

For Christmas Eve, they had a pretty quiet shift. Two motor vehicle accidents, only one requiring transport to hospital, and a case of indigestion posing as a heart attack—which meant that when they got to the hospital, they had to wait around forever in the hallway with that patient because other people hadn't had quiet nights at all and all the Emerg beds were full. They were already an hour into overtime, just shooting the breeze with their patient who'd totally recovered, but still didn't have a bed so he could be confirmed as fine, when her phone dinged.

Jake: Merry Christmas.

She stared at the text message for a minute. Matt shot her a curious look, and she waved him off, drifting down the hallway for some privacy.

He didn't send her many text messages. His last one before this one was the thank you for the ride. Before that, two brief messages from their overnight in London when they took turns sitting with Olivia in the hospital. She scrolled back further. It didn't take long to get to the year previous, and then his first message to her, a generic one.

Jake: This is my new number—Jake.

Nine text messages in total.

All the feeling she had for him, the overwhelming need for him, and they'd only ever exchanged nine text messages.

She was starting to think that the man wasn't capable of opening up. Maybe this plan was futile and nothing would spark his interest beyond a latent *she's hot* kind of thing. But it didn't stop her from responding.

> **Dani: Same to you.**
> **Jake: Matt says you're working with him this week.**

She glanced down the hall at her temporary partner.

> **Dani: Yep.**
> **Jake: Stay safe.**
> **Dani: Thanks.**

And that was that. He didn't text again. Their patient got a bed, they turned their bus over to the next shift, and she went home to a surprisingly sweet Christmas breakfast with her parents and brothers. The single ones, because Rafe and Olivia decided to stay at their place until dinner. Then she hit the hay.

Sleep came swiftly, but with it came dreams of Jake and a different kind of text message. Dirty, secret texts.

***All I want for Christmas is you*.**
I'm yours, however you want me.
***Naked, bent over the hood of my truck*.**

She woke up with a start, a warm ache pulsing through her torso. She grabbed her phone and made sure that she hadn't overslept. When she noted her alarm wasn't set to go off for another hour, she slid back under covers, willing Dream Jake to come back and finish what he'd started.

Dream Jake proved much more agreeable than Real Jake.

CHAPTER FOUR

The last thing Jake wanted to do was go drinking.

But Olivia had cornered him during what was supposed to be a work meeting and spun a tale of Rafe needing to get out. From where Jake sat, his best friend had a beautiful woman at home and a wedding in four days. What did he need to go out for? He'd survived being shot. Life was good.

She wouldn't take no for an answer, though, so he found himself driving through a glittering winter wonderland to the other side of the narrow peninsula. The Green Hedgehog in Lion's Head was the only pub in the area, and they did a good job of it—great beer, good music, nice atmosphere. If he was any other guy, it would be his regular haunt. God knew that his brothers certainly spent enough time there, but it wasn't his scene. He didn't really have a scene, other than being a part-time soldier and building a business.

Matt used to insist on dragging Jake out. When Rafe and Olivia foolishly divorced, Matt pinned his wingman sights on Rafe, but that hadn't worked out very well considering the other man had never fallen out of love with his wife. And now they were back together.

Together. That's really all Jake had ever wanted.

How the fuck had he managed to stuff up whatever he might have had with Dani?

That night five years earlier had been the first opportunity—the night he'd replayed a million times over, wondering if he should have kissed her. Instead he'd walked away. Then she'd come back from college with a boyfriend the following year, and instead of waiting for that to fall apart, Jake had thrown himself on the first plane to Afghanistan, leaving his business in the hands of his newly retired father. Coming back from that tour of duty with a few demons hadn't helped, and neither did Olivia and Rafe splitting up. Dani dated other people. He dated other people, although not as often as she did.

He couldn't, even when she gave him the cold shoulder over and over again.

Giving up hadn't been easy. Or maybe it had been and he'd convinced himself it was hard.

He had regrets a mile long, but none were as sharp as the knowledge that Dani had stood in front of him three weeks ago and told him she still wanted him. Made him admit he still wanted her too. And again he had dropped the fucking ball.

Ryan's feelings mattered. Of course they did. But nothing mattered more than Dani, and he'd lost sight of that somewhere over the years. She was right. He'd put her last for far too long. That had to change.

So spending the night out with her brother didn't seem like a great use of his time. Not when he had a mountain to climb to get back into her good graces. He'd have one drink, then step outside and call her.

He parked beside Rafe's truck, sighing as he recognized both of his brothers' trucks in the parking lot as well. Small fucking world. Of course Matt and Sean would be here, too. And Tom Minelli's SUV was tucked in the corner of the lot.

Something niggled at the back of his brain. Something he should have paid attention to, because it wasn't until he stepped inside and unzipped his parka that he realized Dani was there too. He drank in the sight of her in a tight red t-shirt and jeans as she poured her scary-as-fuck oldest brother a drink from a pitcher on the table. *Zander*. The man made Rafe look like a kitten when it came to protecting their sister. The only Foster/Minelli missing from their generation was Dean, and he was working tonight. He wouldn't show up unless one of them caused a bar fight. Which just might happen if Jake took the bull by the horns and threw himself at Dani's feet.

Maybe tomorrow…

He cursed under his breath and made his way to the bar. It took exactly seven seconds for one of his brothers to barrel into him.

"Left your knitting for the evening?" Sean slung an arm across Jake's shoulders. "Come on, we're going to play pool in the back."

Jake slid a look back at the two tables that had been pushed together for their group. Matt and Dani stood up, but Rafe and Olivia stayed in their seats. "I'll sit with Rafe for a bit. Maybe join you soon." If soon meant never. Dani bent over a pool table? He could see how that would unfold—Zander would spear him with the nearest pool cue.

"Your loss, man. Matt and Dani are going to play Truth or Dare pool. Should be hilarious seeing steam come out of Zander's ears when he hears how his little sister—"

Jake backhanded Sean in the chest. Hard. "Don't talk about her like that."

"It's not me, man. Jeez. It's *Dani*. She practically has a dick."

The hell she did. Jake gritted his teeth together and ordered a pint of lager. Sean disappeared, muttering something about *old men* and *no fun* under his breath.

Rafe, Olivia and Tom were mid-Boxing Day shopping debate when he joined them at the table. "It's like Black Friday in the States," Tom muttered before draining his glass. "No way is it worth it to get trampled to save thirty percent on a flat screen."

Olivia shook her head madly. "No one gets trampled here. And it's *fun*."

Rafe chuckled and pulled his bride close so he could kiss her forehead. "This is why the Internet was invented."

"It's true. I did some online shopping on our way to Mass on Christmas Eve." And she looked damn proud of herself, too.

Jake made a noncommittal grunt and held out his glass. "Well, happy holidays to all, shoppers and boycotters alike."

They all clinked to that, and Tom changed the subject to something they could all agree on—the weather, and how spring could come any time now. Too bad they had a solid three more months of blizzards ahead of them before that happened.

Jake did his best to ignore the raucous laughter spilling from the back room. Tom brought him another beer when he refilled his own glass, and it didn't take Jake long to down his first and that one as well. He'd have to come back for his truck in the morning at this rate.

Matt sauntered back into the main room, heading straight for the bar, where he ordered what looked like enough shots for a celebrating football team. Jake ground his teeth together as he watched the bartender pour bright red something into a row of shot glasses, then start mixing another concoction as his younger brother chatted her up.

Olivia got up, and Rafe leaned across the now empty chair between them. "Work pretty slow now?"

Jake blinked back to the conversation at hand and shrugged. "Got a couple of interior reno jobs on the go. Starting a bathroom next week that I'm going to do myself."

"What's wrong?"

"Nothing."

"Bullshit. Tiling is your therapy."

Jake snorted. So what if this bathroom had a floor-to-ceiling penny tile walk-in shower? "Just missing being on the job site is all."

"You doing okay? Talking to the Fenichs?"

"Yeah. They're hanging in there."

"Olivia says they're still planning to rent their cottages out for the movie shoot." In the fall, Olivia had been poached by film producers to be a local location scout assistant, and had turned the part-time job into a jill-of-all-trades full-time position, including organizing housing for the people who would soon descend on Pine Harbour for the filming of what sounded like a big-deal movie.

"Yep. They'll head south in March."

"Ryan's okay with them being gone from the kids for a while?"

"Honestly? I think he'll appreciate the space. Lynn's life insurance looks like it'll pay out, so he can take as much time off from work as he needs."

“He’s holding up better than I would.” Rafe looked across the room, and Jake followed his line of sight. Olivia had stopped to talk to some locals at another table. Her eyes crinkled at the corner, her smile was genuine and stretched ear to ear. She was a beautiful woman, inside and out. Jake looked back at Rafe, who wasn’t trying to mask the stupid lovesick look on his face at all.

“If you had kids, you’d find a way to be strong for them.”

“Yeah. We’re workin’ on that.”

“Yeah?” Jake kept one eye on Matt and the bartender, who was now writing her number on a piece of paper. Jesus, his brother could flirt his way in—and out—of any girl’s bedroom.

Rafe nodded. “We’ve wasted so much time. And all the barriers we had before…they don’t matter as much as having lost each other. Now we know for sure that we’ll always put each other first.”

Jake shifted his attention away from his friend. No way could he look Rafe in the eye right now, not when those words made him think of Dani.

It would be one thing if he'd fallen for her now. No one would blink. But the truth was that he'd fallen for her when she was seventeen. And he'd been twenty-five. For that alone, he deserved to be dragged out back and kicked in the kidneys a few times. They could add a few black eyes for the fact that he'd loved her all this time and slept with other women.

Matt carried the shots back to the pool hall now, and Jake stood up, muttering something about Zander. He didn't wait for Rafe to respond.

He thought about getting another beer. Then he heard a shriek of delight and strode across the pub to the back room just in time to see Dani slam an empty shot glass down on the table and plant a wet, smacking kiss on Matt's cheek. His brother waggled his eyebrows at

Dani—*Jake's* Dani—and it was a miracle he didn't knock the kid out.

What the ever-loving hell? She giggled, but then sighed as Matt caught sight of Jake and waved. She glanced toward him, picking up her pool cue. "You here to play, Jake?"

Her words were sharp and layered with meaning. And even barbed as they were, they were a bit of her attention just for him. No one else knew what was growing between them. "I'll watch for now."

She shrugged and moved around the table, nudging Matt out the way with a hip bump. "If you don't get in the game…"

"Leave the old man alone," Sean interjected. "If he wants to sit on the sidelines, that's his prerogative."

Jake schooled his features into a calm mask, but from the quick look Dani shot him before she leaned forward to take her shot, she knew that landed. “Jake’s not old,” she said softly as she lined up her shot.

“Sure he is. Old and lonely. Next thing you know he’ll be yelling at kids to get off his porch.”

Matt joined in on Sean’s ribbing. “Why do you think he built his house out in the country?”

Dani took her shot, an easy sink in the corner pocket, but missed her next attempt.

Matt hooted and lifted another toxic red drink in the air. “Truth or Dare, baby girl. Truth. Or. Dare.”

Dani licked her lips and slid a sideways glance in Jake’s direction. “Truth.”

Before either of his idiot brothers could ask her a question he didn’t want *anyone* to hear the answer to, Zander stood up. “I’m going to head back to the table.”

Jake didn’t move.

Sean lined up his shot, then paused there. He glanced up at Dani with a wicked grin. "Smallest dick you've ever seen."

"Yours," she shot back readily, and thankfully everyone in the room knew she was kidding. Didn't help Jake's jaw unclench at all, though.

"That's a lie, Minelli. Take a penalty shot and fess up."

She tipped back her drink. A red drop clung to her lip as she righted her head, and Jake wanted to lick it away.

"I can't answer that honestly, Matt. You know we've got patient confidentiality laws." She brought her hand to her mouth, catching the errant drop then licking it off her fingertips.

"Spoilsport. That's not what we meant and you know it."

"It's all you're getting from me this round. Your turn." But for all the restraint she showed in her words, over the next few rounds she kept touching his brother. A hug here, a hand on the forearm there. Confused, frustrated, and getting absolutely nowhere, Jake stood up and beat a path of retreat before he blurted out that he needed to talk to Dani in private.

She shot him a matching confused look of her own as he ducked out. What did she expect? That he'd join in their weird game and Truth-announce that he'd always wanted to bang her?

No. They needed to talk. Share a lot of shit. But it was going to be in private.

The next half hour sped by in a blur. Zander bought him a beer and tried to talk to him about security services in the area. Olivia graciously moved the conversation in another direction, but Jake still felt like a shit for not caring more about Zander's questions.

A flash of red caught his eye as Dani appeared, Matt and Sean right behind her. Matt snagged her elbow, pointing to the table, but she shook her head and nodded to the bar instead. And when they got there, she perched herself on Matt's knee. His brother—who was surely going to die before the end of the night—laughed and ordered them a new pitcher.

Well, Jake wasn't going to be drinking anymore tonight. He shifted his chair so he could keep an eye on the bar and leaned back, legs spread wide.

Olivia came back to the table just as Rafe noticed where Jake was staring. "What the hell are those two doing?"

She made a soothing noise as she rubbed the back of Rafe's neck. "Ignore them. They're just blowing off steam from a hard couple of days of work."

"She's sitting in his lap," her fiancé growled. He narrowed his eyes in Jake's direction. "No offence, man, but your brother is a walking sex machine. I don't want him anywhere near my sister."

Neither did Jake.

"They work together," Olivia said dryly.

"That's different." This time it was Jake who was unable to hold his tongue. "At work she's wearing a uniform." *Not a thin little t-shirt that he could see her nipples through.* But he couldn't say that out loud. Fuck, he shouldn't have said anything.

Olivia shoved a bowl of pretzels at him, and he wondered how much she knew. Girls talked, right? Would she keep that from her husband?

Dani twisted around and whispered something to Matt, who tapped her on the ass as she wiggled away. Jake barely kept a snarl off his face as he watched her head to the back of the bar.

"Gotta hit the little boys' room," he muttered after a minute, shoving away from the table. He could have sworn that Olivia snorted before pressing against Rafe and suggesting that they dance.

The back of The Green Hedgehog was a warren of hallways and the washrooms were at the very back, in a quiet hallway that led to an exit and an unused staircase to nowhere. There'd be decent warning if someone came through the swinging doors from the pub. It wasn't the place for him to lay his heart on the table, but he could take another stab at an apology—and this time, he'd be the one bravely talking about feelings.

Or something.

He leaned against the wall and crossed his arms. It didn't take long for Dani to come out, and she pulled up sharply when she saw him.

"Having fun tonight?" That wasn't exactly *I'm sorry* or *we should talk*. He needed to work on his apologizing skills.

She gave him a bland stare. "Sure."

Bland, his ass. "Gonna go home with Matt?"

"Would that be a problem for you?"

He pushed off the wall and stepped into her personal space. "You know it would be."

She glared at him, giving up the too-cool-for-school attitude. “I know that *now is not a good time* and you just want to be friends.”

“That was three weeks ago.”

“It’s not like we’ve talked since then,” she said, her tone softening but still wary.

“You want to talk now?”

“I don’t want you to be playing Truth or Dare with my brothers, that’s for damn sure.”

She shook her head. “You shouldn’t have left so quickly, Jake.”

“You definitely wouldn’t have liked it if I stayed.”

“Would you have gone all caveman and carried me back to your den?”

Maybe. Not answering seemed the safest bet.

Her face softened and she almost smiled. With her lips. Her eyes were still dead serious. “What were you afraid of hearing?”

Anything that might make him lose control. Anything about her being with someone else, which made him a total hypocrite.

“I wish you’d stayed.” She licked her lips, leaving a shiny wet path that he wanted to feel against his skin. “Maybe it’s time for you to stop hiding from the fact that I’m a grown woman.”

Deja vu washed over Jake and he shook it off. They’d had this conversation a dozen times in his imagination. He wasn’t going to blow his chance to have it for real. He glanced down at those damn pointy nipples for a second before dragging his gaze back to her flushed face. “I’m painfully aware of that fact, gorgeous. Have been for eight long years, I promise you.”

She crossed her arms like she knew exactly where he’d looked and she wanted him to look again. He ignored the sweet swells her arms plumped up on offer for him and stared her in the eye instead. Which was good, because her next words slashed through his gut. “I wasn’t a woman eight years ago.”

And right there, crackling between them, was the truth of why he’d fought this for so damn long. “You looked like one. And I kept my hands to myself.”

She leaned in, lips parted. Still wet from where she’d licked them. God, he wanted to taste her more than he wanted his next breath. “I didn’t want you to.”

CHAPTER FIVE

Heat radiated between their bodies—almost close enough to touch. Not close enough at all. Dani's mouth was dry, her palms were clammy, and if someone came down that hallway in the next few minutes, she couldn't be sure she wouldn't knock them out.

"I'm getting that message loud and clear," he said roughly. "I hope it's not too late for me to tell you that I heard what you said at Ryan's. What you're saying now. You were right. I should have found a right time a hell of a lot sooner than now."

"I've been really mad at you," she admitted.

"I know. With good reason. But you've got my attention now."

"Because I flirted with Matt?" She lifted her chin. *Please let the answer be no*.

"Because you've always had a slice of it. Always. Now I'm blocking everything else out."

She felt more than saw him lift his hands and oh-so-tentatively cover her hips with his long, capable fingers. Hands that could build houses and defend a nation. Hands she'd only had on her body once, in the most innocent of ways. How could he doubt she wanted him to hold her? "I want more than a moment in the back of the Hedgehog."

"You've got it." He touched her hips, almost tentatively, but there wasn't anything weak in the way he held her. Just slow, like he was giving her time and space to tell him to stop. That wouldn't happen.

"But you were right about one thing." She swallowed hard. This was difficult to admit. "I don't think we should tell anyone. Not yet. Not until we know…what this is between us."

He studied her face for a moment, then lowered his head toward hers. This time he didn't pull up short and kiss her forehead. He ghosted his lips past hers, a hot brush of breath sending a shiver through her body as he pulled her tight.

"Come home with me," he rasped against her cheek. Against the base of her belly, she felt the swell of his erection and as she slid her hands up his hard, broad chest, his heart thumped against her fingertips. God, she wanted to. They needed to be alone, and for more than a few minutes.

But her entire family was a hallway away. They'd both been drinking…

"I can't," she whispered, arching into him. "Not tonight."

He sighed, clearly thinking through the same logistics. "When?"

"I'm working tomorrow night. I traded a shift to get New Year's off for the wedding."

"Breakfast?"

"At the diner where everyone knows us?"

"Come to my place. I'll cook," he said, like he planned to do very naughty things with food. She didn't object—in principle.

But real life meant other considerations needed to weigh in as well. "I'll need to take a nap before my shift."

He nudged his nose against hers. "Then we'll take a nap together."

Hot, molten lava poured through her body at the promise of curling up in a bed with Jake. She couldn't suppress a small moan, and Jake pulled her even tighter against his body. He glanced in each direction down the dark hallway, then pulled her to the far end, right next to the emergency exit. He settled his back into the corner and pulled her against his body. They were mostly in shadow, but his face was close enough to hers that she could see him clearly.

The look on his face made her want to strip off all her clothes. "I was jealous, you know."

She wrapped her arms around his neck, melting into him. "It was nothing."

"My brother touched your ass. That's not nothing. And Truth or Dare? That was evil."

She could feel his fingertips pressing just below the waistband of her jeans like possessive brands. "Zander was there too. It was completely innocent."

"Did Olivia lure me out tonight to watch that?"

Were the shadows deep enough to hide the flush that crept across her cheeks? "Maybe."

He edged one hand higher on her waist, sliding under her t-shirt, finding bare skin. He stroked back and forth, back and forth, raising goosebumps that she could feel all the way down to her toes. All the while he stared at her like they had all the time in the world.

"At some point they're going to notice that we're both missing."

"I want to kiss you first." He said the words quietly, but with a burning intensity.

She pressed up on her toes, bringing her mouth to within a hair of his. "Then kiss me."

He groaned and nipped at her lower lip.

IT WAS hard to think with Dani pressed against him. His cock strained at the fly of his jeans and his heart felt like it was going to thud out of his chest. And he was afraid once he started kissing her, he wouldn't be able to stop.

"Should we wait?" She pulled back a bit, but no way was he letting her go.

He tightened his hold on the hips that had fuelled so many of his fantasies and spread his legs enough to tug her right into his body. "God, no."

He needed more hands for this. He wanted to touch her everywhere. He skated his palms up her sides, his dick pulsing as his fingertips grazed her bra on the way to her face. Shaking with equal parts nerves and restrained need, he cupped her chin, bringing their mouths together. He wanted it to be sweet and memorable, but at the first hot lick of her tongue, he was lost.

With a growl he shoved his hands into her hair and deepened the kiss, tasting as much of her as he could find. He dove deep with his tongue, satisfying that primal need to be inside her, stroking against her tongue as she hungrily sought her own satisfaction in the same way. He cupped the back of her neck with one hand as he sent the other one in search of her hip again. He couldn't get her close enough, not where he needed her, so he spun them around, sliding her against the wall at the same time as he fit one of his thighs between hers.

Dani wrapped her arms tighter around his neck. Her breasts pressed into his chest and he'd just shifted his body enough so he could get his hand between them when the swinging door clapped. She recognized the sound before he did, because she shoved him back and squirmed past, darting into the unlit staircase just before someone with heavy footsteps stopped behind him.

"Jake?"

He recognized Zander's voice. Instead of turning around, Jake leaned against the wall. He was still reeling from that kiss, and painfully aware that his body was still playing catch up to the change in plans. "Hey. Beer's gone to my head a bit."

"You seen Dani?"

He shook his head, a million thoughts thudding through his brain. He'd seen her, felt her, tasted her. And now lied about it all. Not the way to start a relationship.

Behind him, Zander cleared his throat. "You want a drive home? I was hoping we could talk more."

Jake needed to sober up, fast. And get rid of the hard-on that wouldn't die. He turned slowly, shoving his hands in his pockets. "Sure thing. Let's go get me a Coke and you can tell me what you're thinking."

As he followed Zander down the hall, Jake resisted the temptation to glance back. He might have been the first to voice concern about what others would think, but Dani had been clear—for now, whatever was between them was secret.

She came out to the bar area a few minutes later, her cheeks still pink and her gaze very much *not* on him. She headed straight for Matt, an action that he understood even while it scraped him raw. Instead of staring at her, he turned back to Zander and pretended to care about his questions about security system providers in the area. "Yeah, there's a market for more expertise, sure. The options here are basically the national alarm companies."

"I've got a buddy who moved to Fort McMurray and he's got a good business set up. I'm going to visit him in the spring..." Zander kept talking, but Jake drifted away again. Dani and Matt were heading back to the table now—and they were holding hands. Was she trying to kill him?

But when they sat, she took the seat opposite from him, and Matt sat on the other side of Zander, eager to get in on the security chatter. Jake let them go at it and pulled out his phone. He knew he was being rude, but he couldn't concentrate on anything right now.

Something nudged his leg, and he jerked his gaze up. Dani smirked into her glass and slid her foot higher up his leg. He scrolled to her name in his contacts list and tapped out a message.

> **Jake: That's playing with fire.**

Her phone vibrated in her bag and she pulled it out. Then she yawned as she looked at the screen, even as her toes hooked behind his knee. She set her phone down without responding and grabbed a handful of pretzels before turning to her sister-in-law to start a quiet conversation about the wedding.

He slid her another look, and this time she nudged the bowl of pretzels across the table at him. She blinked at him innocently as she ever-so-slowly raked her foot down his calf. She was playing *footsie* with him. And it was giving him another hard-on.

"Whatcha thinking about, Jake?" Dani waved a pretzel at him and he jerked his head as if to say, *bring it*. She lobbed it through the air with decent aim for someone who claimed to be tipsy, and he snapped his hand up to catch it.

"Just planning my day tomorrow. Important breakfast meeting."

"Oh yeah?" She smiled, a little quirk of the lips that made him want to toss the table aside.

"I thought you were taking the week off?" Matt helpfully interjected, leaning between them to grab the bowl of pretzels.

"Change of plans. This is a meeting I've been trying to land for a long time."

"Sounds like a great opportunity," Rafe added, and Jake decided there were six too many people at the table. Since he couldn't very well tell them all to fuck off, he yawned, mimicking Dani's earlier faked gesture.

"It will be. I'm going to bring my A-game. Listen, I'm zonked, and if I'm going to come back in the morning to get my truck, I should get going."

Tom shook his head. “Zander can drive your truck. I’ll follow you guys and then collect him from your place.”

Dani nodded vigorously. “Sounds like a plan. That way you can put all your attention in the morning to your…meeting.”

He flushed at the way she hesitated, then lingered on the last word like it was something filthy. *Jesus*. He hid his face as he pulled on his coat. He tossed some cash on the table, then made his goodbyes without looking anyone in the eye.

Zander talked about his security business ideas the whole way home, and Jake gave him as much of his attention as he could muster. Anything to avoid thinking about the man’s little sister, and all the *attention* she wanted him to pay to her the next morning.

DANI WENT HOME with Rafe and Olivia instead of Matt, although it didn't really matter. They drove back to Pine Harbour in a caravan. She thought she'd gotten off scot-free, but when Olivia pulled up in front of the Minelli house, Rafe got called in by their mother to grab another tray of leftovers. And Olivia took that opportunity to snag Dani's jacket sleeve, holding her in the car.

"What the hell happened with you and Jake tonight?"

Dani pressed her lips together. "Nothing."

"The eye-fucking across the table was *scorching*. I'm a little turned on, I gotta tell you."

"Ew, don't." Dani sucked in a ragged breath, then lied to her best friend. "Just more of the same push-me, pull-me routine."

Olivia gave her a weird look. "I don't know. Something is changing between you guys."

Yeah. Now she knew what Jake's erection felt like. "Wouldn't I tell you if something did?"

"Maybe. Maybe not if it was big and scary and right before my wedding." Her friend offered a nicer smile than Dani deserved. "Whatever you're doing, or not doing…I suggest you don't go anywhere near each other in public again for a while. A few more performances like that and even the biggest dunces would sort it out."

Dani made a noncommittal face as Rafe returned to the car and she made her escape.

She found her parents sitting in the kitchen having a late-night cup of coffee with some fresh biscotti. "Is this decaf?" she asked her mother, slipping the cup from Anne's hands.

"It is." Her mom offered her cheek and Dani dutifully kissed it before taking a big sip. Then she handed the mug back.

"You kids have fun tonight?" her dad asked.

"You know Zander's close to forty, right?"

Her mother gasped and her father laughed.

"Bite your tongue, Daniella," Anne said. "He's thirty-six. And I was practically a child bride."

"Total double standard, then, that you still call us kids."

"Says the woman still happily living at home. You'll understand when you have children."

"Someone has to eat all the food you make. Do you want me to move closer to work? That would be easier for me…"

"Shush, that's enough teasing." Her mother stood and smoothed her hand over Dani's cheek. "You're on night shift tomorrow?"

Dani willed herself not to blush. "Yes, but I'm going in the morning to pick up some last minute bachelorette party supplies. I'll nap at the station."

"I don't know why she needs another bachelorette party." And just like that, Dani watched her mom go from loving to…

something less than loving. It saddened her that her mother never warmed to Olivia.

"She doesn't. But Pine Harbour doesn't have a ton of entertainment options, so we're using the excuse to drink some wine. Don't worry about it."

"You don't need to take it like that."

"Well, you didn't need to say it like that, either, right?" Dani kissed her dad on the head, then gave her mom a one-armed hug. "I'm off to bed. Love you both."

She took a shower, then crawled into bed. When she couldn't fall asleep right away, she reached for her phone. Jake's message still displayed on the screen, and she swiped in.

> **Dani: How early is breakfast served at Casa Foster, anyway?**

His response came immediately.

Jake: Your brothers are still here, or I'd say right now.
Dani: That's tempting.
Jake: You need your rest, gorgeous.
Dani: Oh yeah? For what?
Jake: I can't type that out in front of your brothers.
Dani: Should I call you instead?

A minute later her phone vibrated in her hand and Jake's name lit up the screen with an incoming call.

"Hey, you."

"I stepped outside. Of my own house in the middle of winter."

She smiled to herself. "Poor baby. Sounds cold."

"Cold is the last thing I'm feeling right now."

"What exactly *is* on the menu tomorrow morning?"

"You." His voice—and words—did spectacular things to her insides. Wicked, impossible things. "How early can you get here?"

"I'll probably wake up at seven."

He asked her a few more questions, about what she liked to eat and how long she'd need to nap in the afternoon. It was a surreal conversation, planning a date with Jake after all this time, and she couldn't help but worry that it wasn't actually going to happen. He'd get cold feet and she'd wake up to a text of regret. But his voice was thick with anticipation, a rich wash of eager words spilling through the phone lines, and when they hung up, she hugged her phone close and shut her eyes. Morning couldn't come fast enough.

CHAPTER SIX

Dani had a permanently packed overnight bag, for when she got stuck at work unexpectedly in a winter storm, or on the rare occasion she was asked to work split or back-to-back shifts. And since she lived with her parents, any social sleepovers had to happen somewhere else.

But this was different. For one thing, she didn't know for *sure* that she'd need her toothbrush. Or a change of clothes. Dawn broke over the horizon as she left the house, reminding her this wasn't a typical date.

On the other hand…it was Jake. And he'd kissed her last night. Pressed her against the wall and urged her to ride his thigh. It was a safe bet they weren't going to have coffee and croissants.

She'd woken up with a solitary butterfly fluttering pleasantly in her tummy. By the time she turned into his driveway, there had to be a billion of them, and they all seemed to be telegraphing serious reasons for her to have doubts about this.

What if after all this time, it's awkward and weird?

What if we're not sexually compatible?

What if it doesn't work out?

But before she'd even turned off the car, Jake had the door open for her. It had to be ten degrees below, but he stood there with the door open waiting for her. Like he couldn't wait a second longer to see her, and she'd needed that. She hustled out of the car, grabbing her bag, and as soon as she was within grabbing range, that's exactly what he did.

She laughed as he shoved the door shut and pressed her against it, kissing her softly and thoroughly. The perfect mix of soft and firm, his lips worked their magic on her until she was breathless and far too hot.

"Let me take my coat off," she said when they broke apart for air.

"I'll do it." He tugged on the tab of her parka and holy crap, he managed to turn unzipping her jacket into foreplay as his hot gaze followed his hand down her body. He shoved it to the ground and pulled her hard against his body again. "Are you hungry?"

"For food?" She wrapped her arms around his neck and kissed his scruff-covered jaw. She loved his beard, and the sculpted face beneath it. Her small breasts already felt heavy and they were wearing too many clothes. Food could wait. "Not in the least."

He groaned and slid his hands under her shirt. "Should we talk first?"

"First? Like, before we get naked?" She moved her mouth down his neck, sucking gently and then not so gently as she reached his collarbone. His skin tasted unbelievably good, like freshly showered man with a sprinkle of salty sweet something extra. Was this what fantasies tasted like? She was pretty sure she'd died and gone to heaven. "Take your shirt off."

"So that's a no to talking?" He rumbled the question under her mouth and hands, and followed it with a laugh as she bit him on that delicious muscle that connected his neck to his shoulder. Like all of his muscles, it was perfectly defined and made for nibbling.

"You think we should talk?" She broke away from him, panting, and peeled off her own shirt because he hadn't done as she'd instructed. His eyes dilated and he raked a dark look over her skimpy bra and all the bare skin she'd just revealed.

"Probably." The word came out as a strained growl before he grabbed her bottom and hoisted her in the air.

DANI SHRIEKED and wrapped her limbs around him as Jake carried her up the stairs. All his carefully considered plans of making her breakfast and talking about their history and hopeful future disappeared when she took off her top. Primal need pulsed through his veins as he carried her to his room—the room he'd built hoping one day he'd share it with her, at a time when he thought that a stupid pipe dream.

He'd built it anyway.

And this morning he'd put clean sheets on the bed because he wasn't an idiot. But he was supposed to make her breakfast first.

He strode across the room and set her on the bed, following a heartbeat later after whipping off his own shirt. She arched into him as he threaded his fingers into her hair, holding her still for another kiss.

Her hands roamed over his body, and he held himself above her to allow full access. Her touch made him flex every muscle in her path and left a wake of pebbled skin behind, brewing a strange intoxicating sexual tension. Like he wanted her to tease him forever and ever, but he also couldn't wait until she found the button on his jeans and the erection straining behind it.

Her legs slid through his, then she froze and pulled away from his mouth with a gasp. "My boots!"

Fucking winter. He reluctantly stood and tugged off first one boot, then the other. He paused at the side of the bed for a minute, chest heaving, and before he could climb back on top of her, she'd clambered to her knees and made her way to the edge.

"Hey you," she whispered, an echo of their phone call the night before. "You coming back?"

A faint tremor shook his hand as he stroked her cheek, then traced a line down to her bra. Maybe he had stood there for more than a moment. His head was spinning and his throat was full of gravel. "Don't want to move too fast."

If only he could get his hands and mouth to agree. He dipped his head and breathed in the smell of her neck as he stroked her slim curves and willed himself to slow down. It was so much better than he'd ever imagined.

"Do you have any idea how long I've wanted to do this?" Dani asked, lacing her fingers through his. She brought their hands together to her bra strap. He lifted his head to watch as she used his finger to nudge it off her shoulder. He matched the gesture on the other side, staring into her eyes now, and the depth of want he saw there mirrored his own. But he also saw strength, and a surprising raw honesty that matched her words perfectly. "I'm terrified this is a dream and I'm going to wake up before we get to the good stuff."

She slowly reached behind her, and he didn't know where to look first. The hypnotic bend and flex of her shoulder as she worked at the back clasp of her bra, or those dark hazel eyes flecked with the tiniest dots of gold. Or lower, right between their bodies, where any second her breasts were going to come into view. He fought to keep his gaze on her face until she laughed and tossed the bra aside. "It's okay, you know."

"What?" he asked hoarsely, feeling like a virgin all over again.

"You can look at them." She leaned in and danced the barest of kisses across his mouth, and he shuddered as her nipples grazed his chest. She cupped his jaw, then brought her lips to his ear. "I want you to look at them. Touch them. Kiss them. You know what, Jake?"

His cock strained at his jeans, almost painfully now. He knew. He was positively vibrating with the knowledge that she wasn't a girl anymore. She was a grown woman who liked sex. Who'd come over to his house at the crack of dawn to finally do this with him and he was fucking it up. He groaned and swept her backwards, tumbling after her. He palmed one of the most beautiful breasts he'd ever held, and stole the rest of whatever she was going to say with a deep, searing kiss.

She wasn't a girl anymore, and he wasn't a nervous teenage kid.

"What, Dani?" he asked after gently biting her bottom lip, now wet and glistening and more than a little swollen. She panted up at him as he lazily circled her nipple with the flat of his palm. "What else do you like?"

Her tongue peeked out between her lips, then she smiled, showing him that she'd caught her tongue between her teeth. She inhaled sharply, then slowly stretched her arms over her head, pushing her breast into his hand. "Everything," she said with a sly grin. "Sucking. Licking." Her cheeks turned a darker shade of pink that made him harder than granite. "Biting. Gently."

Damn. That unexpected edginess sliced right under his skin and hooked him in. "I can do that, gorgeous." He kissed her hard, hungrily, then scootched himself lower and braced his forearms on the bed, bracketing her torso. He sucked one rosy peak into his mouth, then let it go with a pop before doing the same to the other one. He repeated the back and forth until Dani was moaning in a regular, breathy pattern, adding in all the things she said including the edge of his teeth. Gently. Then he shifted to one side and slid his hand down the flat of her stomach and into her jeans. "This okay?"

She lifted her hips, tilting her pelvis to welcome his fingers. He found her slick and ready, and that was it. The last vestige of his control slipped away and Jake took her mouth at the same time as he rocked two fingers deep inside her body. The shudder that wracked her body matched his own. The wetness coating his hand as he fucked her with his fingers told him there was a time for foreplay, and it was later. Before round two.

Right now he needed something rougher and more primal. He sure as hell hoped he wasn't alone. The sweet, heady scent of sex swirled around them as he reluctantly withdrew from her tight, hot sex and peeled her jeans down her legs. In turn, she shoved at his pants too, and he barely had time to grab the condom from his pocket before she stripped him and took his erection in hand.

He thrust into her grip, rough jerky movements because he wasn't capable of finesse right then. She stroked him firmly, squeezing at the base and then again around his crown.

Squeeze, stroke, squeeze. Stroke. Stroke. Squeeze, stroke, squeeze. Jake growled and shoved her legs apart, and Dani pulled their sexes together, rubbing herself against the underside of his cock as he fumbled with the condom at the tip.

“Let me do that,” she whispered, and he braced himself over her, his forehead touching hers as she sheathed him, her fingers now slick with his pre-come and her wetness as well, and the lubricant from the condom. It all felt impossibly good and yet still like pure torture, because he wasn’t inside her.

It was all he could think about. Every muscle in his body twitched to cover her with his heavy weight. To surge inside her and mark her as his. And when she brought them together, not just touching, but actually notching him against her swollen, shiny pussy, he thought he’d died and gone to heaven.

Jake had a long history of enjoying sex. He’d lost his virginity at fifteen and spent the next ten years doing everything he could to get into girls' pants. But for the last eight years, he'd only truly wanted one woman.

Now she was here, in his bed. And it was a different kind of first.

"Dani. My Dani…" he ground out her name as he slid deep, filling her and being filled himself. Her warmth imprinted on his skin. Her lips marked his chest and shoulders and neck as he thrust slowly, barely holding himself back from rutting against her like a bull in heat. But she was so damn snug, and he was bigger than he'd ever been before. This had to be good for her. He needed to hold back.

She echoed him, whispering his name as she wound her legs around his hips. One slid higher, her heel digging into his ass, and the other tangled with his thigh as she lifted her hips to meet each of his strokes. One of her hands wrapped around his neck and he welcomed the invitation to get closer. Everywhere she touched, his skin sizzled with awareness, and as they hurtled together toward something that felt slightly out-of-control, he didn't care at all that this wasn't slick or practiced.

Losing his mind never felt so right.

Dani's lips found his and she licked her way into his mouth, curling her tongue around his. Her kiss was frantic and all-consuming, feelings he understood completely, and he groaned into her.

"So close," she panted before sucking his lower lip. "Can I get on top?"

He tumbled sideways, gripping her hips tightly so their connection wasn't broken as they rolled. Like a sphinx, she curled her spine up and sat proudly on top of him for a few seconds. This angle was different, and oh so fucking good. Still hot. Still tight. Still impossible slick. But now there was this gentle weight, too, and he could *see* all of her.

As she started to ride him, he stroked his hands up her hips—the hips he'd wanted for so long, and now he knew they felt even better than he imagined. Soft skin stretched over firm muscle. A small curve of a belly in between, all nipping in to a tight waist and a long, slim torso above that, with those breasts.

He cupped them, rolling his thumbs over her nipples. She tipped her head back and glided one hand down her body to where they joined, her fingers dancing over those dark curls he'd only touched briefly.

Next time he'd go slow and take his time getting to know all the secret spots of her body. Every single part of her fascinated him, including how pink she turned as she neared orgasm.

As if her little gasps and tight, peaked nipples weren't enough of a clue, she told him she was close, over and over again, and he took that as his leave to drive hard into her. He moved faster and faster beneath her as his impending release curled inside him, drawing tight like a pinball plunger. When she came, she ground her pelvic bone against his, her fingers trapped between their bodies, and almost by accident he let go and followed her into the blinking lights and stuttering free fall of spilling himself inside her.

"GOD. THAT WAS...." Dani took a heaving breath, then covered her eyes as her cheeks warmed up. She'd lain next to Jake for a few minutes, neither of them speaking. Well, first she'd lain on him, then he'd nudged her just to the side so he could deal with the condom, but he hadn't let her go far. His arm bound her to his side with fierce determination—like she'd run away from him.

Ha. She wasn't going anywhere. But as she started to talk, to reassure him, she was flooded with heat and she got a bit tongue-tied. It wasn't that she was embarrassed about sex—she was an adult, and sex was fun. But that hadn't just been sex. That had been… animalistic fucking, at points. And crazy tender making love at others. The combination was overwhelming.

"I got a bit rough and manhandle-y there," he muttered.

"Like when you flipped me? God." For a good Catholic girl, she was taking the Lord's name in vain a lot. But after what they'd just done… there was a bit of a naughty Catholic girl in her, too.

"Sorry," he said gruffly, and she laughed.

"No, it was *awesome.*" She laughed again. "Wow. What the hell were we waiting for?"

It was the wrong thing to say. He froze, and so she stilled as well. Should they talk *now*?

"It's not like this was a known option," he said quietly, and guilt lanced through her gut.

No, for the better part of two years now, Dani had been the one to throw up road blocks. She owed him an apology for that, but where to start? That was probably a conversation for another time, when they had clothes on.

"I'm glad we're doing this now," she said. It wasn't as much as she *could* say, but it was something.

"Me too." Under her ear, his heart thumped slow and sure, and she relaxed against him. "I should feed you."

Right on command, her stomach grumbled. He drew her close for a slow, gentle open-mouth kiss that made her nipples tingle, then rolled away. She lay there for a moment watching him move around naked. Did he know how gorgeous he was? His body walked that perfect line between lean and bulk. Long, sculpted legs, covered in an even dusting of light brown hair that had felt delicious against her skin. More hair at his groin, and as he slipped on his jeans—commando, which made her pulse race—she followed the narrowing trail of curls up his flat abdomen to his wider, bulkier chest and shoulders. His arms were made of steel, she'd known before he'd gotten naked, but now she could really take her time and appreciate just how strong he was. There was so much to look at. Including his tattoos. He had a maple leaf on his chest, and when he turned around, she saw the Latin script that matched the same markings on her brother's back.

She climbed off the bed, needing to touch him. She pressed her hands to his back, then followed that with her lips. Curved between his shoulder blades, across his spine, the words *Fratres In Armis* . Brothers in Arms. Her brother Tom had the same memorial marking, from the same tour in Afghanistan. Jake had left soon after she moved home, and when he returned, he wasn't the same.

Surrounded by military men, Dani wasn't oblivious to what happened in war. Zander had nine overseas deployments under his belt between Bosnia and Afghanistan. Tom just had the one tour, same as Jake, and Rafe had only gone to Dubai for a training mission. But they all talked, and sometimes they didn't notice she was in the room. She knew something had happened when Jake and Tom were there, something had gone wrong—more than the usual fucked-upedness of war. *Friendly fire*, they called it, although there was nothing friendly about bombs being dropped on a convoy from three thousand feet in the air. She shivered, sad for the soldiers killed in the lead vehicle, and grateful that Jake and her brother had been a few vehicles back. Tom had been injured, a concussion and a broken arm. Many had been hurt worse. Jake had been physically untouched, somehow, but the way her brothers talked about it, that hadn't been a blessing for him.

She smoothed her hands down his back, then slowly walked around him until she found the maple leaf tattoo on his right pectoral muscle. She kissed him there, just above his nipple, then licked that dark brown nub because looking at it made her mouth water. He shuddered and pulled her against his body, his hands cupping her ass cheeks.

“Let me make you breakfast before you get me hard again.” He kissed her hard and fast, gave her bottom a final squeeze, then grabbed his t-shirt off the ground and handed it to her. “Here, wear this.”

It was deliciously big on her, and smelled like him. She loved it. Leaning over, she snagged her jeans, looking for her underwear that got yanked off with them in their hasty lovemaking. But Jake slid his hand around her arm and pulled her upright.

“Nothing else. Just the shirt.”

An unexpected thrill chased through her body. “That’s…hot. Naked girl in your shirt fantasy, check.” She quirked her lips and sashayed past him, heading for the stairs.

From behind her, Jake growled. "I have a lot of Dani fantasies, brace yourself."

She paused at the top of the stairs and glanced back at him, loving the way he raked his gaze up and down her bare legs. "I've got a few Jake fantasies of my own, don't worry."

He advanced on her and she ran down the stairs, laughing.

CHAPTER SEVEN

He caught her in the kitchen and kissed her until she was breathless and aching to be filled again, but after easing her back against the breakfast bar, he set about actually making breakfast.

Who needed food when there was a six-foot-plus sex god at one's disposal? Her stomach, apparently. Jake glanced up when it gurgled again, then grabbed a muffin from a plastic tray and shoved it into her hand. "Eat this."

She ripped off a chunk and slid it into her mouth. Lemon cranberry. Yummy. She glanced around the gourmet kitchen. It was well lived in, with a stack of papers at one end of the counter and small appliances tucked along the backsplash. Jake might have built this house as a showpiece, evidence of his craftsmanship, but he'd turned it into a real home. She liked that about him—that his house wasn't just a place he put his head at night.

"What are you thinking?"

"You cook a lot." She pointed to the tomato he'd just finished slicing. "You've got vegetables and muffins in your house. All the time."

He laughed. "You don't?"

"Well, sure, but my mom is a chef. If I lived on my own…" Well, there was a reason she didn't. "In college, I lived on ramen noodles and cheese strings."

"Me too."

She frowned. Had she known that Jake had gone to college?

He gave her a pained look, as if he could read her mind. "I think you were ten when I left for school. I was only gone a year. It wasn't for me."

She blushed and changed the subject a bit. "So then you went to work for Mike?"

"Yeah. Just seasonally the first couple of years."

Now her memories were sorting themselves out again. "And you went overseas."

He nodded. "Yeah."

"Just the two tours?"

Another nod. "When I came back from the first one, Mike hired me on full-time. And then I bought the business, and things were flat-out for a year while I built this place and re-branded, got some new contracts."

"But you'd always wanted to go back?"

He gave her a strange look. “Sure, I guess. I’m a soldier, even if it’s just part-time.”

“Why’d you go on that one?”

He frowned, his whole face changing in a split second. A guard went up and his gaze was hooded as he turned back to sausages he was turning in a frying pan.

She regretted asking. It had been an awful tour of duty for him, not date talk. Not even with her. “Can I help?”

“Grab the eggs from the fridge?” he asked without looking at her.

Damn. “Jake?”

He lifted his head, then slid a slow, guarded glance at her. “Eggs, Dani.” He smiled. “I promised to feed you.”

“Actually, I think I was invited here for some sort of construction meeting.”

He chuckled. “You can negotiate me down to a fifteen percent discount on your next renovation."

"Fifteen percent? After I slept with you?" She shoved the eggs onto the counter beside him and planted her hands on her hips in mock outrage. "Give a guy an inch…jeez."

Jake turned down the flame under the sausages and gave her his full attention. "An inch?"

She grinned. "Was it more than an inch?" She tipped her head back and tapped her chin, loving the way he was getting fired up. "I can't remember."

He crowded her against the counter and kissed the base of her neck. "Hell of a lot more. I'm pretty sure I rocked your world for an old guy."

She sighed and wiggled against him as he nudged the hem of his shirt to the tops of her thighs. "You're thirty-three. That's *not* old. It's hot, and you've just gotten better looking each year."

He looked like he liked the sound of that. His lips twisted in a cocky half-smile that made her tummy flutter all over again. “Yeah?”

Oh, he had no idea just how much his maturing looks worked for her. Jake was the epitome of masculine virility, and she wanted to gobble him up with a spoon. “I’ve been watching. And imagining…”

His eyes turned dark as he stroked the front of her bare hips. “Want to tell me one of those Jake fantasies now?”

She bit her lip and spread her legs in invitation, her bare thighs brushing past his denim clad ones. The rasp of rough cotton on her skin felt good, so she did it again, enjoying the dark flare of heat in his eyes.

He cupped her mound as he angled his mouth across hers. “I’m pretty sure this is still my fantasy, Dani.”

She released her lip with a slow exhale, letting her hot breath brush against his mouth. Her heart was pounding a mile a minute, but he'd asked, so… "Is it still your fantasy if you're on your knees?"

"You're not a sweet little kitten anymore, are you?" Jake asked. He was close enough to her face that she couldn't see much past his eyes, but the corners of his mouth curling into a wicked grin couldn't be missed.

"Nope." She breathed hard as he rocked the heel of his hand against her clit.

"I like it. You're a damn tigress, Dani, and I like it a lot." He finally covered her mouth with his, swallowing her first moan, but by the second one he was making his way down her body and on the third one he replaced his hand with his tongue.

He hooked one of her legs over his shoulder and licked his way deeper into her folds. She was soaking wet and already close, if he couldn't tell from the way she was grinding against him, but she didn't want this to be over, either. Leaning back, she braced her hands on the counter and arched her hips into his hands. *His tigress*. That turned her on more than anything, that he truly saw her as the equal she'd wanted to be for so long.

"Oh, Jake," she whispered as he licked up and around her clit, then dove deep inside her. "Your tongue…"

He did it again and again, following that path with a wide lick that wound her tighter with each swipe. And when she grabbed his head, almost without thinking about it, curling her body forward as she held him at her swollen nub…he pulled it into his mouth and sucked, perfectly, carrying her over the edge.

Instead of getting up, he slowly lowered her into his lap, and after settling her within the circle of his steely arms, he stroked her back and legs and whispered all sorts of wonderful things that made her want him all over again. Ridiculously, hot tears threatened to flood her eyes, so she pressed her eyelids shut and kissed him instead. He tasted like sex—like her—and the intimacy of it all could have made her more emotional. But it didn't. Kissing Jake made everything okay.

Better than okay.

"Now can I feed you?" he asked gruffly, and she pulled back, surprised at the emotion in his voice.

"Thank you," she said quietly. "And yes."

He helped her up, then splashed some water on his face before grabbing a tea towel from a drawer. She blushed as he wiped his mouth with it, but he just blithely walked across the room and pitched it into what she remembered was the laundry nook behind the butler's pantry.

She tugged his shirt down over her hips, wishing she had some bottoms of her own. But then Jake didn't have a top on. They were equally undressed…but only one of them was still weak-kneed from an orgasm.

Jake strutted past like a freaking rooster.

"You look proud of yourself," she murmured.

He smiled as he resumed his cooking duties, sliding a new pan onto the range for the eggs. "Make toast, woman."

Dani had a good life, but she'd never had *this* uninhibited intimacy with a lover, and it filled her with an unfamiliar warmth. Two hours into a relationship with Jake—and she had no doubt that's what he intended this to be—and she was happier than she'd ever been before.

So she made toast. A great big pile of it. She poured orange juice into two glasses that Jake set out, then realized he hadn't made coffee. "No caffeine this morning?"

He set the plates on the table, one at the end and the other right beside it, then pulled out a chair for her. "You said you need to sleep this afternoon."

Dani pressed her hand to her chest, touched that he'd thought of that. "If you want coffee,

I'd have half a cup. I can sleep no matter what."

Jake took her hand and pulled her close. She rested her cheek against his shoulder, savouring the warm heat of his skin for a second before he nudged her chin, lifting it so he could kiss her softly. "I can't sleep after coffee, though, and I fully intend to nap with you."

"Are you for real?"

"Warts and all."

"You don't have any warts."

He shrugged. "Maybe a few callouses."

"I like those. They feel good..." She rubbed her face against his hand to prove her point.

Jake laughed, then skimmed his thumb over her lower lip, a more serious look settling on his face. "It's still kind of hard to believe you're here. I don't want to miss a minute of it, even while you're sleeping."

"I'm really here." She kissed his fingertips.

"You're really here." She was starting to recognize that look in his eyes, the one that said *brace yourself for intensity*. He took her mouth again, kiss #546 for the morning, and she lost herself in it. While they kissed, he moved her into the open chair, then slowly licked his way out of her mouth. "I feel like the luckiest man in the world, Dani Minelli."

She pressed her fingers to her mouth as he took his own seat, feeling like the luck was all hers.

After breakfast they cleaned up together, shoulders brushing from time to time. Jake kept looking at her, like he was just confirming she was actually in his kitchen, wearing his shirt, and she knew how he felt.

When he led her upstairs again, and into his spacious master shower, she dropped to her knees and took him in her mouth, intent on returning the favour he'd given her before breakfast. His salty taste on her tongue and his hands in her hair was perfect, but then he hauled her up and pressed her against the tile wall. He ripped open a condom wrapper with his teeth and covered himself in the split second before he slid deep inside her. She squeezed her legs around his hips, but wrapped in his arms of steel, it felt almost unnecessary, like he *had* her, no matter what. And when he started moving inside her, the fingers that were cupping one of her ass cheeks flexed into her flesh, the pressure an anchor in a rapidly approaching storm.

They didn't talk. Heavy breaths and the fall of water all around them were the only sounds as Jake thrust, harder and faster, and as quickly as they'd started, she was done—magically done, with tingling toes and lightheaded wonder at what he did to her body. Jake squeezed her bottom hard as he finished with her, pinning her against the wall as all of his muscles twitched in release.

After their breathing returned to normal, Jake solemnly washed her all over. They wrapped themselves in towels, drying off as he guided her to his bed. An armoire on the opposite wall held a TV, and he snagged the remote before tucking them in.

"It's a bit early for my nap," she said teasingly, cuddling close. And she was probably too sore for anymore sex, although she probably wouldn't remember that if he slid his hand between her legs again. Each time they came together just made her hungrier for him. Spending the next few days apart as she worked and fulfilled her maid of honour duties was going to kill her.

As if he'd just had the same thought, he put down the remote and stroked her cheek. "What are your next few days like?"

"Is that a polite way to ask when we can have sex again?"

He frowned. "Just when I can see you again. In and out of clothes."

She blushed. "Sorry."

"Don't be sorry. I've been a bit of a sex-mad lunatic this morning, but that's not all I want here. Maybe we could go out for dinner or something."

"Should we talk about that? What *all* we want?" They were naked together, in a bed, and all sexed out. Maybe it was finally time to talk.

"I want you," he said, his voice rough. "All of you."

"You've got me."

"I can't share you, Dani."

She was shocked that he'd even need to say that, but it made her think of his *friend* who'd been waiting for him the night of the funeral. And the fact that he'd admitted sleeping with her. *But not that night*. An icky, cold feeling slithered into her gut. "I don't share either," she whispered. "There's no one else, right?"

He shook his head. "No one."

"That woman…the night of Lynn's funeral."

"Tash. She's…" He made a pained face. "She's a friend that I slept with once. Not that night."

He'd already told her that, and she believed him. "Okay."

He held her tighter than before as he flipped through the Netflix screens. Two episodes of *Supernatural* later, she decided it was time to go to sleep.

"Need to grab my phone," she said, tapping his arm.

Jake was already out of bed, and out the door before she could protest. He was back less than a minute later with her bag.

She rolled her eyes at him. "I could have—"

"But I wanted to."

She grabbed his hand. "Hey. Whatever you did, it was before we got together. Let it go."

He gave her a startled look. “What do you mean?”

“It’s starting to feel like you’re trying to be perfect to make up for something.”

He crawled into bed and lay next to her again. “Maybe.”

“Well, stop it. I mean, don’t stop being perfect.” She kissed him. “But this is the start of us. All that happened before… that was *before.*”

A frown formed between his eye brows, and his lips drew into an even more serious line. “That’s not really how I feel about us, I gotta say.”

She gave a helpless little shrug. “I know. Same for me. But I can’t get burned up with jealousy about something you did before today. That’s not a healthy way to go forward.”

His lips twisted together, turning white with the effort to hold back his thoughts.

"What?"

He laughed. "No way can I be that mature about anyone you've slept with."

"It's been a while for me, don't worry." *Like, before her last physical*. She cleared her throat. "Long enough that I've had a clean bill of health from the doctor. And I religiously take the pill."

He stared at her, a wide grin splitting his handsome face in two. "I'll go see the doctor tomorrow."

"I don't mind the condoms. There's no rush. I just thought… it would be nice. If we're exclusive, I mean."

"Tomorrow. First thing. I'll be waiting at the clinic, wearing a placard that says, *this guy wants to screw his girlfriend without any barriers*."

She laughed so hard she hiccuped. "As far as placards go, it's a bit wordy."

He wiped the tears away from her eyes, then kissed her. “Time for that nap?”

HE’D HAD Dani in his arms for ten hours.

Ten hours, two days ago. And since then, she’d either been working or sleeping or planning a godforsaken bachelorette party.

And now she was at Rafe and Olivia’s house, getting delightfully drunk on what looked like an entire wine store from the photo she texted him.

Meanwhile, he was throwing an impromptu poker night for all of her brothers. And his brothers. Plus Ryan Howard, who’d very reluctantly left his kids with their grandparents. But Gloria Fenich had refused to take no for an answer, and she was leaving soon to head south for the rest of winter. Ryan wasn’t so lost in his grief that he couldn’t see the logic in letting his kids have a sleepover with Poppa and Nana. It wasn't the first time, and it wouldn't be the last.

Jake had offered him a room to crash in. That turned into Rafe announcing he'd sleep over instead of heading back to his parents' place, so Zander and Tom decided to stay as well. Matt and Sean bellied up to the scotch, and while Dean promised he'd take them back to his place, Jake knew it wasn't likely. He was the only one who'd given Rafe a send-off last time, and now that the party was underway, it probably wouldn't end until the last man passed out.

The guys had arrived with cases of beer, but the bags of nachos and jars of salsa he had in the pantry would only go so far. After placing a quick call to Pine Harbour Pizza, he took his seat and anted in.

Forty-five minutes later, he'd busted out on all his hands and he was damn hungry. When the delivery guy knocked at the door, he has glad for the break. They ate standing up around the breakfast bar. Rafe leaned in the exact same spot Dani had when Jake went down on her, and he tried like hell not to look as awkward as he felt on the inside.

Sooner than later, it would be all out in the open. He'd stop feeling guilty, and he and Dani could go about building a relationship.

But right now it felt like he was branded with a giant P for pervert.

He wasn't. There wasn't anything wrong about what they did. God, nothing had felt more right in his entire life. But he'd grown up with these men. Spent the last twenty years hearing them curse and threaten anyone who came within ten feet of her.

They hadn't liked any of her boyfriends. Had actively chased off more than one.

And Dani had never fought them on that. A sick part of Jake's soul wanted to believe that's because she was his all along, but life didn't work like that.

But she was his now. And he'd fight them for her. There'd be no running him off.

"Lost in thought, man?" Zander bumped shoulders with him.

"Don't you have a war to go fight or something?" Jake asked before stuffing his face with pizza again. Eating seemed like a better idea than saying anything.

Zander just laughed. "Fly back in a few days, yep. It's been nice to be home, though. Spend some time with this asshole while spends his rehab time getting hitched." He kicked at Rafe, who flipped him the finger. "I missed his first wedding."

Jake tipped back his bottle of beer. "I'll miss this one, fair is fair."

Rafe gave him a surprised look. "You wanted to come tomorrow night?"

"Of course." Jake's answer surprised himself, but apparently not his brothers, who all guffawed. "What?"

"You're such a fucking girl, Jake." Sean shook his head. "I bet you've got a wedding fantasy book of your own somewhere."

He did *not* have a book. He *had* thought of his wedding once or twice, but that's all they were. *Thoughts*. Masculine thoughts of taking a wife and starting a family. He didn't give a shit about place settings or flowers.

"You do, don't you. Holy shit. Where is it?" His youngest brother hooted and hollered as he ran into Jake's office at the front of the house, calling out in a falsetto something about wedding bells and confetti.

Jake just rolled his eyes and grabbed another slice.

"You can come if you want." Rafe held up his hand. "Not your brothers. Just you."

Dean protested lamely, then shrugged. "Nah, that's okay. I'm working anyway. Plus Jake's special."

"Like has ovaries kind of special," Matt said under his breath.

Jake fisted his brother's shirt front. "First... that's enough bashing of women in this house, okay? Having some fucking emotional sensitivity wouldn't go astray if you ever decide to stop acting like a frat boy. Second... you owe me ten bucks for the pizza." He shoved Matt back and grabbed his beer and pizza. "Come on, let's play."

While Dean shuffled, Rafe gave him a quiet elbow. "Seriously. We're staying at the Harbour Inn. A Justice of Peace is going to marry us at six, then we're going to the steakhouse for dinner. Everyone would want you there. *I* want you there. I should have asked sooner."

Dani wouldn't want him there. Not yet. And Rafe wouldn't if he knew...

But Jake wanted to go. For his best friend.

And because he wanted to spend New Year's Eve with the woman he loved.

CHAPTER EIGHT

Dani was already crying and they hadn't left the hotel suite yet.

"You gonna be okay?" Olivia laughed gently. "I'm not crying yet, don't get me started."

The photographer Dani's parents had insisted on hiring kept snapping away, and Dani thought for the umpteenth time that day that eloping made a lot of sense. So many feelings for what was just another day—it's not like Rafe and Olivia were going to be different tomorrow than they'd been yesterday. Plus the cost. And no one looked good with mascara running down their cheeks.

It was really about how silly she looked crying over the whole thing. Dani hated crying. At least she wasn't alone, Olivia's sister Mina had wet eyes too. She'd just ducked into the bathroom to reapply her concealer.

"It's just that you guys…the divorce, and the fighting, and now you're back together…" Dani sniffed and dabbed at the corners of her eyes in a vain attempt to not mess up the professional make up they'd paid too much money for. "And now I'm ruining it."

"The wedding or your make up?" Olivia touched her cheek. "Both are still perfect."

"Why aren't you crying?"

Her sister-in-law just smiled. "I cried all my tears around the shooting. This is the happiest day of my life. I'm all good."

"You should market that in pill-form."

"I'll get right on that."

"I'm glad you're going to be my sister again." Dani fluttered her hands in the air and took a deep breath. "No offence, Mina."

"I never stopped seeing you as my sister, baby girl."

"I know. Now turn around, let me smooth out your skirt."

Olivia wore a tea-length, champagne-coloured strapless gown that made the most of her short, curvy figure. Her long dark hair was sculpted into a retro half-up, half-down do. Dani's hair wouldn't hold the pin curls in the same way, so she'd flat ironed her hair instead, and while she liked her figure-skimming black cocktail dress, she didn't hold a candle to the bride.

As it should be.

"Ready to go find our mothers?"

Olivia shuddered. "Do we have to?"

Dani laughed. “Yep.”

“Damn.” Her sister-in-law pointed to the box of flowers that had been delivered earlier. “There are two corsages for them. Maybe I can give those to them while we get some pictures? Oh, shit. The boutonnieres. Can you take those over to Zander’s room?”

“Of course.” Dani blew her an air kiss, grabbed the smaller tray of flowers and pins for the men, and opened the suite door. In swept their mothers, right on queue. Dani was grateful for the escape as the photographer started barking out positions for the women to receive their flowers in a totally orchestrated way. Ahhh, memories.

The guys were getting ready one floor below. There was still an hour to go before the ceremony, and Dani decided to take her moment of privacy to call Jake. There was a small landing just beside the stairwell with a padded bench. She set the flowers down and double checked that the hallway was empty before dialling. He picked up right away.

“How’s everything in bridal land?” The second she heard his voice, she relaxed. She hadn’t even realized she was tense.

“Good. A little overwhelming, which…I dunno. It’s good. Olivia is gorgeous and happy. I’ve been tasked with taking Rafe his boutonniere, so I thought I’d sneak a phone call to you.” She hesitated before adding, “I miss you.”

“Tomorrow, I’m all yours.”

“And I can’t wait.” She twisted the tear-stained Kleenex that she really needed to throw out. Except she’d need it again during the ceremony. Now she understood why ladies carried lace handkerchiefs.

“Hey, are you okay?”

“Would you believe that I need a hug?”

He laughed quietly in her ear. “Is that a big deal for Dani Minelli to admit?”

“Mmm hmm.”

“Where are you? Can you ask one of your brothers for a hug?”

“I’m sitting on a bench down the hall from Rafe and Olivia’s suite. I haven’t gone down to Zander’s room yet. And a brotherly hug isn’t what I’m looking for.”

“Ah.” His voice was rich and warm, and exactly what she needed.

“Okay, I’ve gotta go find my brother. I’ll sneak another call later. I like hearing your voice.”

“And I like hearing you say that. Be happy, gorgeous.”

Feeling more balanced, Dani grabbed the flowers and ducked into the stairwell—where Jake was waiting for her on the landing hallway down to Rafe’s floor. He’d shaved and put on a suit, and her body immediately responded to the nearness of him—in the good, nipple-tightening, aching thighs kind of way, but also the terrifying *oh my God, everyone will see me want him* kind of way. Her heart hammered away in her chest as if underlining the latter point. “Jake…”

“Be happy, gorgeous,” he repeated, holding out his hand.

Darting a glance all around, she descended the flight of stairs and took it, because even if he was the cause of her panic, he was also the cure. “What are you doing here?”

“Rafe invited me yesterday.”

“And you didn’t think to warn me?”

“This was more fun.” His eyes glinted with humour, but she wasn’t feeling it.

“How am I supposed to spend the evening around you and not let everyone in on our dirty little secret?”

Narrowing his eyes, he took the cardboard flower tray and dropped it on the ground. Then he pulled her close and skimmed one hand up her body as the other palmed her ass in a possessive brand that made her core clench in appreciation. She cursed her womanly bits for not caring that the caveman routine was… caveman-y. Ergo, not cool.

"Don't say that like being dirty together is a bad thing," he muttered, kissing her jaw. "You look amazing. I can't wait to get you out of this dress. Please tell me you've got your own room. I couldn't book one, they were all full."

"I do. And that's not helping." She gasped as he dropped his hand down the back of her thigh only to slide it up again under her dress. Between them he was thick and ready, and she needed him to kiss her even if they didn't have time for anything else. "I can reapply my lipstick, you know."

Barely were the words past her lips before he pulled them together, his tongue tangling with hers in an erotic kiss. All around them, her family was readying for a wedding, but alone in the stairwell with Jake, all she cared about was the electric connection between their bodies.

"You drive me crazy," she whispered against his lips as they both sucked in ragged breaths.

"You make me crash weddings," he muttered back.

Laughing quietly, she kissed the corner of his mouth. She literally couldn't keep her lips off him if given half a chance. "You said you were invited."

"I may have started the conversation that led to Rafe inviting me."

"We can't…I mean, we need to play it cool tonight. Not touching me. I might spontaneously combust."

He nuzzled her neck. "Can't have that. I'll be good. Until the end of the night. What room are you in?"

She winced. "320. Right next door to Tom."

He pressed his lips against the curve of her ear. "Then you're going to have to be very, very quiet when I'm licking you later."

A flame-thrower would have had less effect on her than those words. White, prickly heat flooded her from head to toe and between her legs, fresh wetness soaking her panties. *Gonna have to change* those *before the wedding*. She gaped at him as he pulled back, adjusted his tie, and winked before jogging back down the stairs.

Toward Zander's room. Where she was going.

Oh, no. No, no, no. This wouldn't go well at all. Or at least, not until the end of the night. She pressed a hand to her belly and allowed herself a moment of shiver-inducing rewinding of Jake's last words before she shoved them to the back of her mind.

JAKE TOOK a perverse pleasure in the way Dani couldn't look him in the eye when she entered Zander's room a few minutes later. With pink cheeks and still swollen lips, and in her little black dress, she was the prettiest bridesmaid he'd ever seen.

She handed out the small bundles of flowers, pinned on her father's boutonniere, then made herself scarce again.

Pretty soon the photographer showed up, then it was time to head to the small atrium for the ceremony. Zander produced a flask and they all had a toast to the groom as they filed downstairs.

The gentle strains of string music greeted them as they filed in. The officiant was already there, along with a staff person from the inn. Rafe handed over a small ring box just before his mother and Olivia's mother arrived and announced "the girls" were just outside. Rafe stood a little a taller, and Jake was hit in the gut with an intense desire to be in his shoes.

Swinging his gaze to the door, he held his breath as first Mina, then Dani, walked through the door. He should have been paying attention to Olivia following them in and taking Rafe's hands in the middle of their semi-circle of family members, but all Jake could see was Dani.

Her long, dark hair swung over her shoulders in a shiny, hypnotic curtain and her slim black dress looked innocent until she took a step and it clung to her hips, and all he could see was the shape of her body.

They may have only shared one day together so far, but he'd already memorized her every curve, and the brief taste of her in his arms in the stairwell had lit up that knowledge with sparklers and neon highlighting. The width of her hips and the pert roundness of her breasts, topped by nipples he could still taste on his tongue. The way her skin pebbled under his touch and how wet she got when he stroked her just so.

The music faded away and the Justice of the Peace looked back and forth between Rafe and Olivia. “It’s not every day that a couple contacts me and say they want to get married —again.” That got the expected laugh from the small group, and he smiled at the couple. “I understand that you have done a lot of talking, and soul searching, as you made this decision to bring your paths back together, and share a life again.

It is fitting that you choose to begin this union tonight, surrounded by those closest to you. But like all New Year’s resolutions, know that there will be stumbling blocks. As you’ve already discovered, marriage is hard. Making it last is even harder.

Rafe and Olivia, you two know that better than anyone, and after talking with you over the last few weeks, I believe you take these vows seriously and with a depth of understanding and meaning that greatly impresses me.”

The officiant looked down at their hands, already clasped and covered them with his own.

“Rafe, do you come to this marriage to Olivia with renewed commitment and intent?”

Jake watched as his friend smiled widely. “I do.”

“Will you love, honor and cherish her in sickness and in health, for richer or poorer, for better for worse, and forsaking all others, be faithful to her as long as you both shall live?”

“I will.”

“For real this time?” Everyone burst out laughing, and the officiant raised his hand. “They asked me to say that.”

Rafe nodded. “For real this time.”

Then it was Olivia’s turn, and she repeated her “I do,” “I will,” and “For real this time” with the same broad smile her husband had. Beside her, Dani blinked a few times, her eyes wide like she was holding back tears, but she held it together.

Grabbing his pocket square, Jake tapped Tom on the shoulder and pointed to Dani, handing over the folded cotton. Tom handed it to his sister, who smiled a polite thanks until Tom pointed back at Jake. When her gaze hit his, the room lit up for just a second, a warm, bright connection that she broke as quickly as she'd made it.

He jerked his attention back to the ceremony just as Zander handed Olivia's ring to Rafe.

"Liv, I give you this ring as a symbol of my love." He slid it on to her left hand.

Lifting her hand, Rafe kissed his wife's knuckles, and Dani's tears started to fall. Jake was going to tease her about that later as he kissed his way down her naked body.

Olivia stroked Rafe's cheek before taking his ring in her fingers. "Rafe, I give you this ring as a symbol of my love." She nudged it over his knuckle.

Clearing his throat, the officiant murmured something quietly, then Rafe and Olivia spoke at the same time. "With these rings, we wed. This time, forever."

"You may now kiss the—" He cut himself off, because Rafe already had Olivia hauled against his body, his arms around her waist and hers around his neck, their vow-sealing kiss very much in progress. "Yes, the bride."

They kissed twice, then whispered *I love you* to each other before the Justice of the Peace turned them to face everyone else. "I now present as husband and wife, again, Rafe and Olivia Minelli."

Cheers led to hugging, and by the time everyone had kissed the bride, two servers had come into the room with trays of champagne and appetizers. Dani stuck to the opposite side of the group, no matter which way he turned, and he didn't press her to be closer. When she caught his eye after murmuring something to Mina about how good the champagne was, he lifted his glass and made a mental note to have a bottle sent up to her room. He wanted to drink it off her body.

The photographer coordinated a bunch of family photographs, then whisked the couple outside for some wintery wedding pictures while the rest of the group headed to the attached steak house.

Inside the dining room Rafe and Olivia had reserved, they found an appetizer buffet set up and a private bartender—a very pretty bartender.

Tom leaned toward Jake. “My offer for you to stay in my room is now officially rescinded.”

“And what if Zander beats you to it?” Jake tipped his head toward Tom’s oldest brother who’d just pulled a twenty from his wallet and was making a beeline for the bar and the bartender’s tip jar. “He who tips first…” From behind him, Dani laughed, and he turned around slowly. "You like that?"

She nodded. He left a safe four feet gap between them, but he hoped his eyes said it all. *You're beautiful, my Dani.*

A smile told him she got at least part of the message.

After Rafe and Olivia returned, the bride wearing the groom's suit jacket because she'd gotten cold and the groom wearing a shit-eating grin because he finally had his wife back, officially and everything, Zander proposed a toast. Then it was Dani's turn.

"I know Rafe said no speeches," she said slowly, pulling out a thick, spiral bound sheaf of papers with a glossy cover printed with the words *Dani's Really Long Speech*. "But I had to grow up with fart jokes and nobody to play tea party with me, and I missed your first wedding, so suck it."

Jake smothered a laugh as Olivia gave Dani a high-five.

"But I don't need a hundred pages, small point font, single spaced to say everything I want to say about brothers and sisters. If I still just had brothers, I'd do it anyway out of spite, of course. Since Rafe marrying Olivia means that we don't need to carry on our special sister bond in secret, though, I'll cut him a break."

Smiling at her brother now, Dani lifted her glass. "Rafe, despite your dislike of wedding speeches and tea parties, you're a wonderful brother. I'm so proud of you for being an upstanding soldier, a police officer, a community member, son and neighbour. But I'm most proud of you for finding your way back to Olivia. The last two years I've stayed close with each of you, and continued to love you both. So I had a front row seat for the fireworks." She got more laughs for that, but Jake didn't think she was going for a funny punchline. "And Olivia…the first time my brother brought you home as his wife, I was just a teenager, and I didn't have a clue what real love was. Even as you struggled, I could see how much you cared for each other. That you continued to serve him breakfast over the last two years—wanting him close even when you didn't like him…that just underlined all the lessons I've learned from you both over the years."

She cleared her throat and stared at her notes, and all of a sudden Jake realized…she hadn't planned on saying any of this in front of him. *Look at me*, he silently urged her. *Look up and see that I want to hear this. It's not too soon. All these years, you've been on my mind, too. All that I know about love I've measured against how I think about you*.

Her cheeks darkened and she bit her lip, then she started again. "Lessons learned from Rafe and Olivia's Tragic Love Story." She peeked up then, glancing first at her brother and his wife, then quickly at Jake. He winked, and she took a deep breath before continuing. "One. Think seriously about telling your spouse they're wrong. And when in doubt, let them think they're right. Two. Endless patience is probably a good thing. Three. Coffee keeps people together, even after a divorce. Four. Be gentle with each other. And Five…" She stared at the page for a minute, then folded it in half and looked up with a wink. "Beware the small town gossips. And sisters."

Everyone toasted and laughed, but Jake saw that Dani's hands shook as she tucked that sheet of paper into her purse.

As the servers brought in their first course, the table sparked up with quieter pockets of conversation. Before the main course, Rafe's parents spoke. Before dessert, Olivia's mother and sister stood and shared some stories about a young Olivia, before everyone else knew her.

After all the plates were cleared, Rafe rose and lifted his glass. "I'd like to thank you all for coming tonight, and celebrating the end of what we're going to call my dumbass period."

Olivia laughed and shook her head, her eyes crinkled shut. Rafe gazed down at his wife with a fondness that Jake recognized from inside himself, then he set his glass down without doing a toast and moved behind her chair. Ducking his head, he whispered in her ear and she nodded, squeezing her eyes shut even more. Rafe guided her out of her chair to stand in front of him, and he wrapped one arm around her waist and snagged his glass again with the other.

"To our family." His eyes settled on his parents as he finished the toast. "And sticking things out, no matter what."

Everyone offered their cheers, then Rafe handed off his drink to Tom. "I just told Liv that my New Year's resolution is to learn how to dance. That's not going to help me tonight…" he nodded at Zander, who tapped the screen on his iPhone, which he'd hooked up to portable speakers at some point. At the first crooning lines of *Unchained Melody*, Olivia finally started crying. "But we're among family.

And I do love dancing with my wife. So…" He pulled her away from the table, and they swayed to the music as if they were the only two people in the room.

It turned out that Zander had a whole playlist programmed, so next Olivia danced with Alessandro Senior while Rafe danced with Anne. When the third song started, and the groom looked like he wanted his bride back, Jake stood up. He could dance with Dani's mom.

"It's nice to see you here tonight," Anne said as they turned around the room to an older country song.

"When Rafe gave me the opening, I took it."

"You're practically like family." She smiled up at him. "When are you going to start one of your own, hmmm?"

Just as soon as your daughter lets me, he thought with a wince. She wouldn't look at him so happily then. "I'm still young."

"Oh, Jake." She shook her head. "One thing you've never been is young. Not even when you were a hooligan getting in trouble."

"I never got in trouble!"

"College drop-out?"

Oh. That kind of mom-disapproved type of trouble. "Respected business owner?"

She laughed and patted his arm. "You do have that going for you. If you weren't in the army, I'd suggest you maybe think about dating Dani."

Stumbling over his feet, and then hers, Jake had barely right himself before Anne laughed again. "Not really, of course. But I've always wanted her to settle down with someone like you. Not *you*, of course."

"No," he muttered, his heart pounding. "Of course not."

CHAPTER NINE

Dani watched Jake dance with her mother, then Olivia's mother and her sister Mina.

The twinge of irrational jealousy that she felt at the last dance pairing made her grumpy. Mina had a boyfriend, and Jake only had eyes for Dani. She knew this. Could feel it in the way he unerringly found her even as she moved around the room. But she wanted to be in his arms. And when Kip Moore's *Hey Pretty Girl* started playing, she grabbed her wrap. She couldn't listen to that song and be in the same room as Jake right now. It was cold and dark outside, but some fresh air on the terrace would be better than longing for something that only she was holding herself back from.

“Hey Dani, want to dance?” Tom snagged her elbow and spun her around.

“Uhhh…”

Before she could answer, Mina bumped hips with her and slid next to Dani’s brother. “Dani should dance with Jake, not one of her brothers. I’ll take you for a spin.”

And then he was right there, holding out his hand as if to say, *I didn’t ask, and you didn’t ask, so hey, why not?* And damnit, she couldn’t think of a reason why not until her hand slid into his and her body responded with a delicious head-to-toe sizzle.

He settled one hand in the small of her back and wrapped the other around her clenched fist. “Nice speech.”

Dani thought of that piece of paper folded in her purse. “Thank you.” Her voice caught on the words and when he rubbed his fingers up and down at the base of her spine, she wanted to lean into him. Take some of the warm strength radiating off his broad shoulders and wrap herself in his Jake-ness.

“You had a different number five, didn’t you?” She *so* wasn’t ready to answer that question. As her parents danced past, she took the excuse and changed the subject to work but he didn’t let her talk about work for long. “What didn’t you want me to hear?”

His question burned her from the inside out, stealing all her breath. It was way too soon for that. But she couldn’t deny the direct question, and she didn’t really want to. She just didn’t want to overstep the fragile bounds of a new relationship. “It was…about taking a leap of faith.” She swallowed hard. “With someone…special.”

Nodding slowly, he found her ear and made his next words for her alone. “Am I someone special to you?”

She tugged back, needing to see his face—even though she feared everyone around them could read the chemistry between them that arced every time they made eye contact. *Eye-fucking*, Olivia had called it. Dani jerked her gaze away before she got sucked in by the hard planes and cut lines of his face. She looked around the room, but no one was paying them any attention.

“I’m terrified to tell you how special you are to me.” His words brushed back and forth over her skin, a rough awakening of all her nerve endings. “Worried I’m going to scare you away. That this isn’t real.”

“We can’t have this conversation here,” she whispered, pressing her hand to his shoulder in regret.

He eased away from her as the song ended, but kept a firm hold on her hand. The hungry question in his eyes made her shiver. “Dani?”

She shook her head. “I’m not scared.”

A small smile played across his firm lips. “Me neither.”

The party continued for another hour, with silly selfie pictures and more dancing, but Dani and Jake didn’t touch again, didn’t talk either, and it didn’t occur to her until Rafe and Olivia hugged everyone and announced they’d see everyone at brunch in the morning that she didn’t know how to slyly sneak Jake into her room.

It turned out, he had that covered.

He left before everyone else, and when Dani collected her purse and wrap, her room key was missing. She headed for the front desk, where the clerk happily coded her a new one.

Her heart thumped in her chest as she waited for the elevator. Anticipation heated her veins as she walked down the quiet hotel corridor toward her room. And when she slid the key card into the slot and watched the green light blink an erotic welcome, she couldn't hold back her excited grin any longer.

"What are you smiling about, sis?" She froze half a step into her darkened room and turned to see Tom—who must have just stepped out of his own room—giving her a confused once over. "You're lost in your own little world there."

"Long day," she said quickly. Her cheeks were red with guilt, but Tom wasn't really looking at her.

"Zander and I are heading down to the bar to meet that bartender and a couple of her friends for drinks. Do you want to come?"

She shook her head. "Not tonight."

"Come on, it's New Year's Eve. You going to ring in the new year in your PJs?"

She made a noncommittal noise and he waved at her over his shoulder as he headed up the hall to Zander's room. "Come find us if you decide to be fun, baby girl."

She waited a beat, making sure he wasn't going to turn back before she pushed the door open all the way and stepped into the dark—only to be swept into Jake's arms. As the door swung shut, he took her mouth in a slow, decadent kiss.

"I've missed you so much," she whispered against his mouth as his hands caressed her hips and back. He found the zipper on her dress and peeled it off her as she worked at the buttons on his dress shirt. He'd already ditched his jacket and tie, and it didn't take long for them to stumble across the room and roll onto the bed into a half-naked, turned-on twist of body parts. "Tom's gone out for a while."

"I heard." He sucked on the skin at the base of her neck and she arched into him, wanting him to tug her breasts out of her bra and move that mouth a few inches south. "But you still need to be quiet."

"Why?" she gasped as he teased her nipples through the thin mesh cups.

"Because it makes me hard to know you're trying your best to be a good girl."

Moisture flooded her sex as she reacted to all the different layers of that revelation. They all worked for her. *Damnit*. Tonight wasn't the night for those doubts to creep between them. Their first day together had been amazing. Two equally wanting adults coming together. Literally. Their first night was going to be the same.

She slid her hand between their thrusting hips and squeezed his raging erection through his dress pants. "Don't you like it when I'm loud?" She stroked her fingers lower, lighter, reaching between his legs. She cupped his balls, firmly, and he groaned and tipped his face into her neck.

"Fuck, Dani, I'll take you however you want to be taken. But I want to make love to you, repeatedly, and then fall asleep with you, and your family hearing you loudly tell me to lick you *right there* would put a crimp in those plans."

She laughed quietly and rewarded his misery by unzipping his fly. "I do like to tell you where to lick me."

"I've noticed." He nipped at her jaw, then braced his arms on either side of her head. The room was mostly dark, the only light—from the lanterns outside the inn—sliding in between the parted curtains. But she could make out his face, and he looked deadly serious. "You can be completely in charge if you want."

She frowned. No, that wasn't...

If this was going to work, she needed to trust that Jake wanted her, the Dani of here and now. He hadn't given her any reason to doubt that—in fact, as she rewound all their heated exchanges of the last week and the month before that, there was plenty of evidence that she was the only one stuck in the past.

“I don’t want to be in charge,” she whispered, turning slightly beneath him. “I want to be good.”

As she rolled, her hip rubbed against his heavy length and for a minute she was tempted to roll back and just rock him into her body. They didn’t need any games to get off.

But she *didn’t* want to be in charge tonight. She wanted to be taken care of after a long, unexpectedly emotional day. She couldn’t quite convince herself that Jake had come for her—the hunger in his eyes made it pretty clear he couldn’t stay away for his own reasons—but he’d still been there with a hug, and a wink, and a dance, just when she’d needed him.

And now she needed to be a little dirty, and before she’d gotten twisted up in her head, he’d already offered that, too.

He palmed her ass, his fingers curling in toward her heat as he settled beside her. "You drive me crazy, woman."

Dani buried her face in the pillow as he slid though her wet folds. The feeling was definitely mutual.

"Have you been this wet all night? This swollen and ready for me?" He hissed in her ear when she nodded. "I can't wait to be buried deep inside you, gorgeous. I've missed your sweet pussy so much. Missed fucking you. Missed licking you."

With each inflaming sentence, she notched her hips higher, shamelessly presenting herself for him as he stroked her inside and out, sliding his fingers deep before pulling out—making her moan in longing—to squeeze her ass again.

"All the ways I've dreamed of you, Dani…this is so much better." His voice was rougher now, more urgent, and he yanked off her panties, no longer content to have them shoved to the side. They tangled at her knees and he rolled her onto her back, covering her body with his. He was hot and hard and ready between her legs, but after kissing her with a bruising intensity that left her breathless, he moved down her body. Dragging wet, hungry kisses across her skin, the slight scratch of his five o'clock shadow a new and different sensation from the softness of his beard a few days ago, he wound such a magic around and through her that by the time he sucked first one nipple, then the other, into his mouth, she was close to coming for him.

And very, very close to making a lot of noise. He smoothed his hand down her trembling midsection and pressed firmly against her lower belly. "If you want me to keep going, you gotta be quiet."

She swallowed her moan and nodded.

"Breathe," he said, low and thick, just above a whisper. She wanted to do the exact opposite, hold her breath and strain for the peak of ecstasy that felt so close. But he repeated the command, over and over again, as he kissed his way between her legs, and then he licked her slow and sweet, and she knew there was no point racing for her orgasm. He wasn't in any hurry, and he wanted to keep her on the edge of pleasure.

And she wasn't in charge. Letting go felt so glorious. She exhaled slowly, her tension fluttering away as Jake's tongue tripped across her clit and back down into her wetness, a lazy figure eight pattern. He dove deep on the next pass, his nose and chin pressing into her as his tongue slid inside her, and she shuddered against his face, coming apart on her next breath.

"Wow," she whispered. "That's a neat trick. The breathing thing."

"Feeling good?"

"So good."

"Excellent. We're just getting started." He pressed his face into the soft inside of her thigh, then rolled her over again and she let herself be flipped. She was boneless and happy, and her mind was swimming with all the possible next steps. Jake kneed his way between her legs, then coasted his hands over her thighs, bottom. When he reached her hips, he squeezed and lifted, tugging her back into that presenting position. Her sex tightened in anticipation as she listened to him rip open a condom wrapper, and then he was there, filling her up. Ever so slowly, his thick length slid into her body. She pressed her hips up and back, eager to take him deep. Hungry to be stretched from the inside out in a way that satisfied a lot more than a physical ache.

"Three days was too long, gorgeous. So unfair to give me a taste of you and then be busy," he teased, folding himself over her body.

She twisted her face to the side. "I'm sorry…"

“Not fair for you, either.” He kissed her temple, then licked along the ridge of her ear. “Let me make it up to you.”

“M’kay.” She closed her eyes and gave in to the blissed out feeling of Jake thrusting slowly in and out of her as he held her down. She wiggled one hand under her body to find her clit. She didn’t move her fingers, just held them still and let Jake rock her body over them. She could’ve gotten lost in the rolling, sweet orgasm he gave her with his tongue and something told her this one was going to be the same if she just let it come to her.

Jake sped up, moving faster toward his own release, and then he was heavier—on top of her, inside her. He braced one arm beside her head and wrapped the other around her, cupping her breast and thumbing her nipple as he surged hard. Three more thrusts and they finished together, Dani with spots in her eyes and tingles all over. Jake…if she could find her voice, she’d ask him how he was, but from the tight hold he still had on her and the whispered, hungry words she'd vaguely recognized as she tumbled off the cliff, she was pretty sure it had been good for him too.

They clung together, all out of breath and sweaty, until Jake softened inside her and he had to move to deal with the condom. But then he was back, holding on to her again, and she didn't care if she was sticky.

The post-coital come-down felt totally right and not awkward at all with him.

Even when he brought up a conversation she'd never expected to have. "Your mom seems to think you've got a thing against dating guys in uniform."

She cursed her mother for not fully getting her. "I don't have a thing against dating *you*."

"I'm not likely to go overseas again."

Laughing, Dani twisted into his body and ran her fingers through the hair on his lower abdomen. He was hard all over, but right there, where the muscles dipped in a sculpted vee toward his groin, he was ultra-masculine. And two back-to-back orgasms had only made her hungrier than ever for him—all of him. And only him. "That's not why I've never dated a soldier before."

Jake danced his fingertips down her spine. He didn't ask her for more. Maybe he knew without her spelling it out. *You're the only soldier I've ever wanted*. She'd always been careful to never date anyone like him—anyone that worked with their hands or served their country. And if she'd ever met anyone as possessive or intense as Jake was in private, she probably would have run in the opposite direction. Fast. But she recognized those feelings in herself, too.

She'd never been a jealous person with previous boyfriends, but with Jake? She would lose her mind if she ever lost him. If she only had the memory of him owning her, body and soul, while another woman got to live it. Wrapping herself tighter around his body, she pressed a line of kisses up his torso, straight to his waiting mouth.

"Happy New Year," she whispered against his lips.

"You happy, gorgeous?"

She smiled as he nuzzled her cheek. "So happy."

CHAPTER TEN

January came and went. Dani's toothbrush found a permanent presence in his bathroom and at least a few times a week, she slept wrapped around him in his bed.

Jake wanted to ask her to move in with him, but given that she still hadn't told her family they were dating, that seemed a bit presumptuous.

And he wasn't sure they were even *dating*, exactly. They'd gone to Owen Sound once to see a movie, and out to dinner another night in Port Elgin. Both towns safely south of the peninsula, away from prying eyes. A grand total of two dates in more than a month.

Used for sex wasn't exactly what he was thinking, but every time she slept over, he was reminded that he'd built this house so they could raise a family in it.

Dani didn't seem to be future-focused at all. *It might help if you asked her what she wanted*. But he couldn't. He was terrified that her answer might not be the same as his.

And the first conversation they needed to have, before he started popping the big questions, was really, *hey, can I not be your dirty little secret?* But he was a fucking coward, because he couldn't ask her that, either.

So when she texted him to say she was coming back to his place between night shifts, to sleep, he told her to let herself in, but he'd be on the job site all day.

Jake: Sorry I can't get away.

It was a lie. He was the boss. If she thought about it, she'd probably know that didn't make sense. Jake gritted his teeth. She wouldn't think about it. She was totally happy with the easy nothingness of their arrangement.

The way she makes you feel isn't nothing, *asshole.* There was a big part of his conscience that knew he was wrong to be pissed off. But damn it, talking about feelings wasn't anything he had experience with, and when it was so easy—and perfect—between them physically, he selfishly wanted them to magically be on the same page for the rest of it.

Dani: If you make it home for an early dinner, I'll give you a dirty blow job before I leave for work.

He was totally stupid for not thinking that was the best idea ever.

Jake: Tempting, gorgeous.

He stared at his phone for a minute before sending a follow up message.

> **Jake: You could grab takeout and come see me here.**

She didn't respond right away, and he could fill in the silence. *Then your crew would see us together. Two phone calls later and my brothers will know*.

Well, it was fucking stupid that they didn't. That he hadn't manned up and told them himself. That in a month of sleeping together, he and Dani hadn't talked about it again.

They'd been too busy in bed. And on his couch, in his kitchen, and all over his bathroom. He'd been too busy taking bubble baths with the woman of his dreams to notice his grump coming on, and now it was here.

She finally responded.

> **Dani: Maybe.**

That was enough for him to tuck his phone away. He'd rather pretend it wasn't a polite *no*. He grabbed a case of tiles and headed back into the year-round cottage they were renovating for a nice premium—as long as they got it done by the middle of February. A film shoot was coming to town, and all the fancy people needed places to stay. Nice places, with rainfall shower heads and in-floor radiant heating.

Hell, he could appreciate that. And it was a good business to be in, that was for sure.

When he dragged himself home, well after Dani left for her third night shift in a row, and he found a casserole in the fridge with a post-it note on it.

> ***Eat this. Not quite as good as sex, but those houses won't build themselves.***

And a heart. She signed it with a damn heart, which made him feel like dirt. So he ate it and sent her a text of thanks right away.

THREE DAYS LATER, Dani was driving home—to her parents' house, although she was rarely there anymore—after an unexpected day shift. She'd work four nights on, then had a day off before being called in to fill in. She hated those non-weekends, when it seemed like all she did was sleep and do laundry and reset her clock before diving into work again.

Jake had had the day off today, and she knew he was disappointed they didn't spend it together. So she was going home just long enough to grab some clothes.

Her mother was setting the table when she blew through the kitchen. "Do you want some manicotti?"

"Mmm, that sounds good. But no, I'm heading out again."

She got a solid raised eyebrow for that, and she winced.

"Are you going to introduce us to this boy?"

He's not a boy, she thought. "Yes. Eventually." *When I know it's serious*. The last thing she wanted was to get everyone else tangled up in their business if Jake wasn't serious. And although they'd had an amazing month of connecting physically, they hadn't had any further conversations about their relationship since New Year's Eve.

Anne set down the cutlery she'd been holding and touched Dani's arm. "You seem happy."

"I am. And I'm sorry for being vague."

"Go spend a minute with your father before you leave again."

So Dani did that. She got the update on the football scores from Europe, then a lecture about driving in the dark, and finally she escaped with a box of biscotti and muffins.

As it had every time she'd done the same thing over the last month, her heart beat a little faster as she deliberately drove in the wrong direction, heading to the main strip instead of out of town to Jake's house. She looped down to the tiny marina at the harbour, then cut back through the residential neighbourhood on the outskirts of town. A ridiculous play at subterfuge, and one that would end soon.

Dani sighed. *Maybe when I'm not bone tired and just want to fall asleep on Jake's chest*.

Inside she found another person she cared about setting the table—for one. And it wasn't the table, but his breakfast bar.

"Hey," she said quietly, leaning against the archway leading into his kitchen.

He gave her a tired, lopsided smile. "Have you eaten?"

She shook her head. "I should have called…"

He put down his plate of leftover shepherd's pie and came around to where she stood and pulled her in for a warm, comforting hug. "You want to share mine? Or there are two other leftover plates in the fridge. Your casserole or a bowl of chili."

"I really want your shepherd's pie," she mumbled into his neck.

He laughed, a quiet rumble as he stroked her back. "Grab another fork."

They sat across from each other, taking turns stabbing off forkfuls of the potato, meat and vegetable dish. After a few bites, Jake got up and got a can of beer from the fridge, pouring it into two glasses.

He asked her about her day. She asked about his. They discussed their plans for the next day—Jake had to work for part of the morning, but they'd have the afternoon together if the electrician sub-contractor showed up on time. It was lovely and domestic and exactly what Dani needed. Add in the beer, and she was halfway asleep by the time he rolled her onto the couch, turned on a police procedural that she couldn't care less about, and slid his hand under her shirt. *That* she cared a great deal for, because Jake's hands were big and rough and made magic out of the simplest caress.

"So there's this regimental dinner and dance on the fourteenth," Jake murmured against her hair. "How would you feel about coming with me?"

She shrugged, fighting to keep her eyelids open. "I don't know." A whole bunch of other questions crowded toward her tongue, but they felt big and clumsy and she didn't have the energy to ask them.

He stroked her side, not saying anything. She burrowed her head deeper into the deliciously hard pillow that was his biceps, and wondered if maybe they could have sex while they were asleep. Because she wanted to have sex —*always, gotta love the honeymoon period of a relationship*—but also…sleep.

"Do you want to go up to bed?" she asked drowsily. "Maybe some slow missionary position action. Think I can rock your world with my eyes closed?"

He stiffened behind her. “No.”

Frowning, she lifted her head. “No? That’s harsh. A simple, ‘not tonight, baby’ would suffice.”

“Fine. I’m not in the mood, *baby*.” Jake’s words sliced through her sleepiness and she jerked upright, rubbing her face.

“Okay…I think I missed something.”

He stared past her, shaking his head. “Nope.”

“Wow, that’s mature. What’s going on?”

“Absolutely nothing, I’m pretty sure.” He swung his legs around her and stood up. “I’m going to do some work for a bit.”

She watched him stalk toward his office, pain and confusion warring in her heart. What were they fighting about? She gave him a few minutes, but sitting on his couch waiting for him to talk to her—or not—felt weird and wrong.

Standing, she replayed the evening, wondering where it went hinky. Dinner had been nice. Cuddling had been nice. She slowly walked to Jake's office. He was standing at his desk, like maybe he was warring with himself over what to do, too.

She said his name, softly, and he turned and pinned her with a hard gaze.

"What's going on?"

"What are we doing here?"

The question took her by surprise. "Well, I was hoping you'd come to bed and make love to me, but it looks like we're fighting instead."

"Is that what we'd be doing?"

She frowned. "What do you mean?"

"Is it making love?"

"Of course it is." She sighed. *Shit.* "Look, I'm exhausted—"

"Then go to bed."

His tone slammed into her like a ton of bricks, all hard and unwaveringly stubborn. “I was going to suggest I make coffee so we can talk about this.”

“Is there anything to talk about?”

“Well, you seem to think…” She trailed off, not wanting to name the ugly accusation she thought she was hearing in his voice. No. She shook her head. “I’m not going to guess. What are you thinking?”

He stormed toward her, crowding her against the door. “I think it’s been more than a month that we’ve been sleeping together, and nobody knows.”

“Half the town’s population is made up of our various brothers, and I’ve never been in the habit of telling them about my sex life! What’s wrong with wanting to keep this just between us?” She’d thought it was special, their little secret. Now she didn’t know what to think.

"I was under the mistaken impression that maybe we were building toward a real relationship. I didn't realize you wanted to keep having a secret affair." He sneered down at her. "Is that all I am to you? Dirty fucking that you don't want anyone to know about?"

"Hey," she snapped, so pissed off that they were fighting about this—that he'd waited until he was this hot under the collar to bring it up, and that it had boiled over on a day that they were both tired and *done*. But even though she could vaguely name all of *that* as the problem, his words were incendiary and she couldn't ignore them. "I thought you liked *fucking* me now. You're the one who had years of a guilt complex over the attraction between us, not me."

"Then why the hell won't you come to a goddamn ball with me on Valentine's Day?"

She glared up at him, her face blazing. How could he not hear himself? No good was going to come of this conversation. Swivelling, she slid under his arm and headed back to the living room. This wasn't her house. She didn't have a safe place to retreat like he had his office. But she didn't want to leave, either. This felt like a turning point in their relationship—their first fight, their first moment of serious discordance. They could retreat to their own corners, but she couldn't leave. If she did… she worried that would slam shut his emotional gates and it would be another five years of longing from a distance—or worse, forever.

She hadn't known that Jake's heart was this damn fragile. And if he'd just talked to her, instead of letting himself get so wound around the axle…

Cursing under her breath, she grabbed her favourite throw pillow, the red nubby one, and stretched out on the couch. Maybe she should go back in there and try again. Or should she wait for him to come to her?

If only boyfriends came with manuals.

Troubleshooting Problem 3.2. Big Tough Alpha Male Gets His Secret Feelings Hurt.

Solution: Who the fuck knows, good luck with that.

Yeah, a manual wouldn't help.

She sensed him before he stepped into the sitting area and before he said anything. The black cloud he dragged in with him was practically radiating the worst kind of heat.

This wasn't going to go well.

And her fear was confirmed as soon as he opened his mouth. "You didn't answer my question."

"It was rude."

"Then let me rephrase. Is this just sex between us?"

She frowned. First of all, that wasn't the question he'd asked her. A dance? No, she didn't particularly want to go to the formal event with her brothers, as Jake's date. She didn't want anyone to intrude on what they had just yet.

And as for sex… Yeah, maybe it had been just about sex in some ways. But they were still new to each other. What was wrong with wanting to build a relationship up from that foundation of a physical connection? He'd never asked for more, or initiated any deep and meaningful conversations. And now he was springing this on her… She shook her head. "I don't know how to answer that right now. I don't want to say the wrong thing."

"Wrong answer, buttercup. Because I do. And we're clearly not on the same page." He stalked to the door, swiping his work boots on the way. She followed, feeling helpless, and watched as he shoved his feet into them without bothering to do up the laces.

"Where are you going?"

"Anywhere but here." He shrugged into his coat and yanked his keys off the hook.

In all her thoughts of not storming off herself, she hadn't taken into consideration *this* possibility. "But this is your house!"

"And it smells like you now." He stared at her, his gaze hooded and unreadable. "I can't do this, Dani. Not if you're not all in."

"I'm not—" Dani watched in shock as Jake jerked the door open and then closed it just as harshly behind him. "I *am* all in," she whispered to herself.

CHAPTER ELEVEN

Jake headed for his brother's house, but only got as far as the edge of town before he realized he couldn't very well tell Dean what the hell was going on.

And he'd just stormed out on Dani like a fucking toddler. *Shit*. He pulled out his phone and sent her a quick text message.

> **Jake: Don't leave. I'll be back.**
> **Dani: Tonight?**

His gut twisted in guilt.

Jake: Yes.

Instead of Dean's place, he went to his dad's. The Colonel still lived in the rambling century home they'd grown up in, although all four of his sons had moved out.

"Jake, this is a surprise," his father said gruffly after opening the door.

"I was hoping to get something from the attic." Four years he'd owned his own house, and he still hadn't moved his childhood stuff out of the old man's place.

"No problem. Take a few boxes home. Could use the space."

Jake grunted, not up for the usual tug-of-war they did. He liked leaving stuff behind. *The ties that bind a family of emotionally unavailable men.* "Got big plans for the attic, do you?"

"Might think about selling this place, actually."

It was an idle threat. "Sure. Move into the retirement home and take up crocheting."

His father waved him off and returned to his show. Jake didn't bother taking off his boots—another benefit of a testosterone-rich living environment—and headed for his pile of boxes on the top floor. He knew exactly what he was looking for.

In the last few years, he'd made the move to keeping photos on his phone like everyone else, but before he got his first smart phone, he'd kept a small wooden box full of photos on his dresser. It was a fine line between being a stalker and showing her how much—and how long—he'd cared, but he needed to do something and words had failed him already tonight.

They needed to talk, but first he needed to give her something tangible before she gave up on him entirely for being an oaf and a brute.

He took the entire cardboard box labelled ***Jake's Dresser*** and headed back downstairs. His dad twisted around in his recliner and grunted at him. "Your other arm broken?"

Laughing, Jake shifted the box to his left arm, detoured into the living room and held out his hand. Fosters didn't hug unless their football team won the Superbowl—an official Colonel Foster rule. One that Matt and Sean had perverted, of course, but Jake and Dean were the good boys.

Too good. Too well trained. Too repressed.

"Good night, sir."

"Might do ribs on Sunday."

"I'll be here." He cleared his throat. "Might bring someone with me." *God willing.*

"Good. Can she make coleslaw?"

Jake laughed again. *He'd* make a coleslaw and let Dani take credit. Not that she'd want it. "On second thought, she might be busy."

"Get out of here and don't come back until you bring a woman with you." His father turned up the volume on his show and turned back to the National Geographic magazine he'd been reading at the same time.

Jake got out of there.

He'd only been at his dad's for ten minutes, tops, but his truck had already cooled off and his breath puffed in front of him. He barely noticed as he peeled back onto the road out of town. Toward Dani.

Say you're sorry, he told himself. *Mean it*. He would and he did, but it was ingrained in his nature to bristle and argue, and if he did that, she'd slay him.

He liked pulling into his lane and seeing the house blazing with lights and Dani's car parked in front. He tapped his garage door opener and rolled inside. He glanced across the interior of the space. The other side of the garage held some construction supplies he'd randomly unloaded from his truck here instead of at the company showroom on the highway, and his snowblower. All of that could be moved. He hopped out of his cab, snagged the box of stuff from his dad's, and stalked across the garage. The other door opener was on a ledge along the wall, and he picked it up.

He'd stormed out the front door, so instead of slinking in the mudroom, he went out the side door of the garage and up the front walk again. Out like a lion, in like a lion. Just an apologetic one this time.

SHE'D MADE coffee when Jake said he was coming back. Then she lay down on the rug in front of the fireplace—after lighting a fire—and did some deep breathing exercises. When the door swung open, she didn't bother to get up.

He stalked in, clearly looking for her. She watched as his boots went to the kitchen first, and he paused long enough to set something on the counter, then he stomped back to the foot of the stairs. "Dani?"

"In here," she said softly.

God, he was beautiful. Long legs, powerful thighs. She'd never get enough of looking at how he filled out a pair of jeans. And when he crouched, bringing the smell of man and cold winter with him, his face all drawn and serious and unbelievably handsome, it made her heart ache.

"I'm sorry," he said gruffly. "It's been a long day and I unloaded on you."

"How long have you been upset with me?"

He reached out and touched her cheek, and she resisted the urge to cover his hand with hers. To pull him down to the rug and kiss him instead of talking. They made love so easily. Too easily. That wasn't where the problem lay, so it wouldn't be where the solution was found.

"It's probably that I'm upset with myself. Can I show you something?"

She nodded silently and took his hand, letting him pull her up. As soon as she was on her feet he wrapped her in his arms and kissed her softly. “I’m really sorry,” he muttered against her lips.

“Me too.” She stroked his cheek. She missed his beard. He’d been able to grow it out over December because his unit stood down for the holidays, but now he was back in the usual routine of shaving at least once a week for his Army training night. Her clean-cut, upstanding citizen. “I hate that you got the impression that I think this is just sex between us.”

Just saying those words tore her apart. So did the look in his eyes.

“It’s not,” she quickly added. “And I’m sorry if I let my…enjoyment of our physical relationship take precedence.”

Jake just stared at her for a second, then swore under his breath as he spun her toward the kitchen. She barely caught sight of a large cardboard box on the counter before he snagged her by her hips and pulled her hard against him, one hand sliding possessively to the nape of her neck. "Gorgeous, never be sorry about how it is between us. Letting my worries fester? That's all on me."

"Tell me, then." She let herself touch him then, trusting that if she slid her hands under his shirt he'd keep talking.

"I'd rather show you." With his free hand, he reached behind her and rifled through the cardboard box. Finding what he wanted, he hesitated for a minute before pulling back and handing her a photograph.

"It's me," she breathed. It took her a few minutes to place it. She was younger, probably in college, and it was summer. She was standing on a dock wearing a bathing suit and a t-shirt—damp in places, so she must have just gotten out of the lake and pulled it on. And she was laughing, her legs slightly bent, knees together, hands clapped together in glee.

He handed her another one, from a bonfire party. She was holding a Tim Horton's cup and talking to Tom, her lower lip snared between her teeth as she concentrated on what her brother was saying.

The next one was older. Her high school graduation. God, she looked so young, all legs and arms and so damn proud to be wearing a fancy dress even though she didn't quite fill it out. She was staring straight at the camera, and this moment she had no trouble placing. Jake had come over to hang out with Rafe. Her mother had thrust the camera in his hands after telling her brother he needed to change his shirt so they could have a family picture. Everyone else had been busy, and Jake had looked at her like she was the only thing he could see, and he quietly told her she looked beautiful. Dani had floated through her entire grad formal on a high from that moment, even though after he snapped that picture he hadn't been able to look at her again for more than two years.

"Where did you…"

"That one I stole from your parents' place."

She choked back a laugh. “Seriously?”

“Your mom printed a whole stack of pictures from that night. They were on the table, and…”

“Jesus, Jake.” That made her feel…funny. In a good way, but also…

“I knew I couldn’t have you.” His voice was rougher than sandpaper and sexy as hell. “But you were so pretty. And if I couldn’t have you…”

“You’ve been my creepy stalker all these years.” She leaned back enough so he could for sure see the humour in her eyes and the smile on her lips. “How many pictures of me do you have?”

“Just these.” He hesitated. “And a bunch on my phone.”

“You *need* to show me those.” She licked her lips. “There aren’t any naked ones, right?”

He didn’t take it like the joke she’d intended. “Dani, that’s not funny. I’d never—”

"Settle down, hero. I know."

His grip tightened on the back of her neck as he stared into her eyes. "I'm no hero, Dani, but I've always tried to be better than my base instincts."

"Because you were attracted to me when I was a teenager?"

He winced. "Yeah, in part."

"What's the other part?"

"Because Rafe trusted me. I was supposed to be like a big brother to you."

Under her touch, his core muscles rippled as he reacted viscerally to the betrayal he still felt guilty over. The guilt she'd helped perpetuate over the last month.

"I had no idea," she whispered. "I wanted you, too. I *never* thought of you as a big brother. You were always different. Always a man in my eyes, and I dreamed that one day you'd see me all grown up and want me."

He shuddered and pulled her tight against him. She pressed her lips to his neck, the warm, firm skin there, and kept talking. She'd keep reassuring him until he heard it for good. "You couldn't help noticing me, Jake. We've got a thing between us. Not sex. Something unavoidable and deeper than that. You're such a good man. You kept your hands to yourself. Kept your eyes to yourself, too, because I didn't know."

"I worried that you did. That night that I drove you home…"

She crooned a nothing noise against his skin, wanting to soothe him from the inside out. "I wanted you to kiss me so badly."

He didn't say anything. He didn't need to. There was no space for regret between them, and they'd spent enough time dwelling on the past.

"So…we should have talked about us, I guess. Now. Sometime in the past month when I was busy ripping your clothes off."

"I don't want to sound like a whiner. I really like the naked part and don't want to discourage future clothing removal efforts," he said gruffly.

"You're my boyfriend, Jake. I just don't want to share you yet. I told my mom about you today. I mean, not *you*, but that I have a boyfriend and it's…serious."

She hadn't realized how tightly wound he was until his muscles softened under her touch. "I told my dad I'm seeing someone, too. Just now. That's where I went—to get this box. He wants to have a family dinner on Sunday and I told him I might bring someone."

It was such a big step. Telling everyone would be…noisy. Definitely some yelling. And a lot of speculation. *Ugh*. "Okay."

"Okay?" The disbelief rolled off him in waves.

"Well, 'I don't know' went over like a lead balloon for the regimental ball thing, so I don't want to make that mistake again."

"No." He bit the word out like it tasted bad, but he didn't let go of her. "We can do this at your pace."

She rubbed her face against his neck, breathing him in. "My pace would be glacial. I'm so happy right now, I don't want anything or anyone to burst that bubble. I don't want to share you yet."

She didn't want to have to defend their relationship, either, and his mind must have gone to the same place. "It's something we'll have to get over with at some point. But it doesn't need to be dinner or the ball. And when we do it, I'll be holding your hand the whole time."

It was her turn to kiss him, then, and after whispered promises to keep talking—more often and more thoroughly—they went to bed together and fell asleep holding each other.

They didn't make love, but Dani woke before dawn to Jake's hand on her breast and his erection wedge against her bottom.

"Go back to sleep," he muttered.

"You're not making that easy." She stretched, rolling her ass against him, and he groaned.

She rolled over, welcoming him with her whole body. It was fast and simple, and as soon as she shuddered to her hungry climax, he followed with his own.

A quick, hot shower later, they were back in bed. Jake held her close, and at first she thought he'd gone back to sleep, but when she tipped her head back to look her fill at his face, she found his eyes stuck on her.

"What?"

"Nothing." He cleared his throat. "Some shitty regrets piling through my head, that's all."

"No, don't…" She trailed her lips over his jaw. "This was meant to be, just like this."

"I keep thinking if I hadn't gone to Afghanistan, maybe we'd have done this four years ago. Or the year before that…"

How many times had she had the same thought? That if he'd given in to temptation and kissed her that night, maybe there wouldn't have been anyone else. Only…there *had* been others for him. She took a deep breath, then let it out completely.

"I've gone back and forth on saying this, because…well, because you're you. And I'm me, and I know what it's like to be greedy for you. I'm so damn greedy, Jake. I want all of you, every last piece. But I'm glad you weren't my first," she whispered softly. His grip tightened on her hip. "No, hear me out."

"I don't want to think of you being with other men."

"There weren't that many." She smiled into his neck as he stiffened. "But back then…you were experienced. And I wasn't. And if you'd been the one—"

He growled and flipped her onto her back. He stroked his rough, calloused hand over her cheek. "I should have been."

His face was so serious, all hard angles and glittering eyes that she couldn't help but laugh. "No, baby."

"But you're mine."

That just made her laugh harder. She buried her face in his neck. "I know, you dork."

He cupped the back of her neck and arched over her, tilting her face so she could see him again. "Why is that funny?"

God, he stole her breath. A hot, needy rush of feelings swept through her. "Because I've always been yours," she whispered. "Even when there were others, it was never like this." His nostrils flared and she lifted her hand to his cheek. There were things that needed to be said. "No, hear me out. If you'd been the one to take my virginity, then I'd forever be that innocent girl you'd deflowered. And I'm not a girl. I'm a woman. I'm your woman. I come to you as a sexual equal, and I can give myself to you without a power imbalance. And I do give myself to you, one hundred percent."

He arched one eyebrow. “Wow, you’ve really given this a lot of thought.”

She glared at him as he fought to conceal a smirk. “Yes, I have.”

“Did you practice that spiel in front of the mirror?”

“Maybe.”

“Huh.” He gave her a thoughtful look.

She shook her head. “No room for regrets, okay?”

“Easy for you to say. I’ve spent the last five years hating every asshole you’ve dated.”

“They weren’t assholes.”

“Every single last one of them. Especially the one who…”

“His name was Dave.”

“Woman, I’m warning you.” He rolled onto his back and pulled her in to his side.

“He wasn’t very good.”

“That doesn’t make me feel better.” But it did, because he smiled a little.

“You’re the best I’ve ever had, by a country mile.”

He smiled a bit more.

“This is the part where you say the same thing back to me.”

He just stared at the ceiling, a weird grin on his face.

“Jake!” She poked him in the side. “Fine, be like that. It was Halloween, and I was Wonder Woman to his Batman.”

“Enough,” he said softly. His fingers pressed firmly into her arm as he pulled her into his side. “Of course you’re the best I’ve ever had. You’re the only woman I’ve ever loved.”

Shit. Well, that topped everything. “Oh.”

"I'm not going to apologize for wishing you'd never been with anyone else, no matter how much logic you shove at me. I lost my virginity when I was fifteen. You were seven, and it would be another ten years before I even thought of you as anything other than Rafe's sister. I didn't know I should wait for you. Like you say, maybe it's good that we both spent time with other people, I can see that in my head, but I don't feel it in my heart. Because once I fell for you, I knew you'd be the one. Even if you didn't want me, I didn't want anyone else."

Except he hadn't exactly been a monk the last few years. Nearly celibate wasn't the same as totally celibate. But she'd just taunted him with how she'd lost her virginity, so she couldn't rub other women in his face.

Plus he'd just told her he *loved* her.

"Oh." Damn it, she needed to say something other than that, but she couldn't. Hot, prickly tears burned behind her eyelids. She'd been so flippant, so teasing. So hurtful. “Jake, I love you too.”

His arm tightened around her.

“We’ve wasted a lot of time.” Her voice scratched in the semi-dark of his room.

“No.” His voice was equally rough. “Like you say. Maybe it’s for the best. Now we’re equals.”

But even though she’d practiced it—convinced herself of the truth of it—now she wasn’t sure at all that the wait had been worth the pain they’d caused each other.

CHAPTER TWELVE

The alarm clock went off at six, far too early when all Jake wanted to do was hold Dani close. Three days had passed since their fight and subsequent making up. Three days of whispered *I love you*s and tentative Valentine's Day discussions. He'd had his weekly training night the evening before and bought a pair of tickets to the ball. Matt and Tom had both been there when he bought them, and he hadn't had any guilt about who he wanted to bring.

He hadn't told them, though, either.

As much as it was killing him to be patient, it would pay off. And Dani *had* said she'd go with him. It was just the logistics of how and when to tell people that hadn't been sorted out fully. Or at all.

When the snooze period ended and the alarm sounded again, she rolled over him and hit it herself. "Go to work and let me sleep in," she mumbled.

He kissed her head, threw himself into the shower, then reluctantly dragged himself outside. It was hovering around zero, but there was a storm coming. The day before the Karpinskis had a heavy tree branch fall on their roof, and it had busted their attic window. They'd tacked up a sheet of plywood and some plastic, which would hold, but it was visible from the road and they had a Bed & Breakfast.

Jake sighed to himself as he slid into the parking lot at Mac's. Dani was making him soft, not that he was complaining. But being busy with work was never something he'd begrudged in the past. He shoved his hands in his pockets as he hustled into the diner.

Inside he found Olivia Minelli sitting at the counter, drinking a cup of coffee and scrolling through her phone.

"You're up early," he said, sliding onto the stool next to her.

"So are you."

"Storm's coming, may need to close up our job sites mid-day."

"Yeah, I was just emailing with my boss. We were supposed to go out for the day and do a site tour, but they're packing up and heading back to Toronto before the rain comes."

"Rain?"

"Didn't you hear the forecast this morning? Weird front, temperature's going up and then it'll plummet overnight. Looks like we're going to be getting more ice than snow."

He nodded when the new waitress brought the coffee around, and took a couple of long sips while he thought about all that would impact. Couldn't have anyone on the roads early tomorrow, either, not until the salt trucks were out. He pulled out his own phone and quickly composed a weather alert memo to his employees.

By mid-morning, he was glad he'd done that, because the weather was turning quickly and the radar map looked nasty. He made his apologies to the Karpinskis, promised them a new window as soon as the storm passed, and headed to his office for a quick check-in with his clerk before heading home.

Where Dani was still blissfully sleeping.

He stripped off his clothes and climbed into bed.

She woke up and rolled into him. "What are you doing home?"

"Storm's looking bad, so we're hunkering down."

God, he liked how she said home and meant his house. "Oooh, that sounds fun. Board games in front of the fireplace kind of fun."

"Or naked under the covers kind of fun?"

She laughed. "Sure. We can alternate."

His phone rang and he cursed, but she waved him toward it.

"I'll take a quick shower. Find me one of your t-shirts and some work socks to wear."

"Work socks?"

"One of my Jake fantasies. Humour me."

He took the call from Johnny first, then found them both warmish clothes. As warm as Dani could be with bare legs, because she wasn't the only one with fantasies still on the docket. He was going to taste every last inch of her legs as he spread her out in front of the fire—

Right after he answered his phone. *Again*.

This time it was Matt. And the first words out of his brother's mouth did a perfect job of killing Jake's hard-on. "Hey man, is Dani there? She's not answering her phone."

Jake's eyes jerked to the bathroom. "Uh…"

"Look, it's urgent, so I don't have time to play this fucking game. I'm pretty sure you guys are sleeping together, and we need her to come in to work tonight."

"Yeah, she's here." Jake's pulse thumped painfully in his throat. "She's in the shower. I'll get her."

"Thanks. Tell her to call me. She's got a few hours, but the storm is going to get worse, so they want more buses out there overnight."

"Sure." Jake swallowed hard around that growing lump. "Matt…about Dani…"

Silence filled the phone line. His brother cleared his throat. “I don’t think anyone else knows.”

“How…”

“I came by your place last week. Her car was out front. And I overheard her telling our dispatcher about a new guy. I put two and two together and came up with ‘I’d rather not know’.”

“Appreciate the discretion, man.”

“When this shit is over, you guys might want to think about just telling people. Unless it’s just a casual thing.”

“It’s not a fucking casual thing.”

“Good, because Rafe would kill you. And I’d help.”

“Fuck off.”

The shower turned off as he hung up the phone, and Jake yanked on a pair of sweatpants. Then a t-shirt. He had a hoodie in his hands when Dani sashayed into view wrapped in a towel.

"Did you find me some sexy wool socks to wear?"

He laughed. "I did, but I've got some…news."

"Should I read the word *bad* into the pause?"

He jerked his hand toward the bed, gesturing for her to sit. "Maybe. I don't know. Matt just called."

"Is everything okay?"

"He just called *you*."

"Did you answer my phone?" Her voice pitched up at the end of the question, as if to ask *are you a complete idiot?*

Since he wasn't, and he didn't, he just shook his head and waited.

"Oh, shit. He called you. Looking for me." She pressed her lips together and drew the towel tighter around her body.

Jake nodded. He couldn't bring himself to do it grimly, because Matt was a good test balloon. But control was important to Dani, and she'd just realized she didn't have any on this front.

"Work?"

Another nod, and this one he accompanied with the clothes he'd pulled out for her. She tugged on the socks first, then the t-shirt. She ignored the boxers, and stood, holding out her hand. "Coming?"

"You don't want to know what he said?"

"Come tell me in front of the fireplace. If it was more urgent than that, you'd have already told me."

He reached out and took her hand. "I love you. Never forget that, okay?"

She gave him a small smile. "Same." She took a deep breath. "Okay, so that's one down, five to go. I'll tell Sean, you tell the rest of them?"

He smacked her ass playfully. “Sean’s the only one who won’t care.”

“How about that.” She batted her eyes at him.

“You’re okay?”

“With people knowing that I love you? Yeah. I can deal with that.”

DESPITE WHAT SHE’D told Jake, Dani had still been nervous when she drove to the EMS station in Wiarton. But Matt wasn’t there when she arrived—he’d been on the day shift, and was still out on a call. She was partnered with Will Mickelson, and now they were halfway between Wiarton and Pine Harbour, heading for yet another motor vehicle accident—what sounded like a simple slide off the road due to the now freezing and slippery road conditions.

Made getting there a bitch, too. But the call in had been from the responding police officer, not the driver, and they had good information. No need to rush.

The Jeep was off the road, nose down in the ditch at a precarious sixty degree angle. The first responder, an OPP officer, stood beside the driver's open door. He waved them down. Dani grabbed the back board and scrambled down the embankment after Will.

She hung back as the senior paramedic greeted the constable, a guy Dani recognized but whose name escaped her. "What do we got?"

"Conscious female, strong vitals. Some confusion and nausea following a single vehicle MVA. No visible head trauma." They knew that from the call, but it was good to re-confirm the situation on arrival.

Will glanced back at Dani before asking his next question. "Any alcohol or recreational drug use?"

"None observed or suspected."

The woman in the car moaned and Will moved closer. “Hey there. I’m Will. What’s your name?”

He pulled out his pen light and examined her pupils.

“Nat…” She trailed off and tipped her head back, pressing her lips together.

“Can you wiggle your toes for me?” Will nodded as he observed her. “And push down?” It was fucking cold and pitch black, and Dani knew he was doing his due diligence because the backboard would be unnecessary if there was no cause—and on a night like tonight, it would be a shitty way to spend a few hours before hand-off to the ER staff.

But it was still cold and dark, and the sooner they got back in the rig the better.

“Good job, Nat.” He ran through a few more questions, got her to squeeze his hands, then reached in and unbuckled her seat belt. “Okay, we're going to get you out and look you over more thoroughly in the ambulance."

The tow-truck arrived as they crested the ditch, and then the rain started again—it had been a minor miracle that they'd had a break while down at the car. Dani moved the ambulance ahead twenty feet, then they climbed in and got Nat out of her wet coat and covered in blankets.

Even with the extra warmth, she started to shake as shock set in.

"Where are you from?" Dani asked to distract her.

"Tobermory." The northern tip of the peninsula. "I was heading home. It was stupid, I should have stayed in Port Elgin last night."

"Do you have any existing medical conditions?" This question was from Will, who'd finished taking her vitals and running through the neuro tests again.

"Uhm..." She pressed a hand to her stomach. "I'm pregnant. It's early still."

That might explain the nausea. Adrenaline messed with most people. It did an extra trick or two to pregnant bodies. "Do you have someone you want to call?"

She shook her head. "Only my parents, and they'd want to come get me. I'm fine, right?"

Will nodded at Dani, giving her the practice at this spiel. "Given that you're alone, and with your pregnancy, we'd recommend transport to hospital. If someone can't come get you, the hospital can arrange a taxi to take you to your car in the morning. I'll find out where it's going to be towed."

Right on cue, the officer knocked on the back doors. Dani took Nat's purse, and the officer's card and a copy of the accident report. She told him they were heading to Wiarton General just for precautionary measures, then once Will gave her the good-to-go sign, she flipped on the lights and pulled onto the highway.

At the hospital, Will gave a brief report to the triage nurse, but Nat was well enough they didn't need to hang around until a doc saw her. Dani handed over her card as well as the paperwork from the responding officer, and wished her well.

And if Will hadn't gone to grab them coffee, and she hadn't stopped to talk to Nina Henderson, the admitting clerk and a friend from high school, she wouldn't have heard any of the triage assessment conversation. It was supposed to be private. She shouldn't be listening at all.

But then the nurse said, "Right now we're looking at an eight-hour wait, are you sure you don't want to go to Owen Sound instead? Or at least call someone to wait with you and take you home?"

Dani's ears perked up. Partly professional concern—dispatch had nixed the transfer plan, because the labour and delivery triage in the larger centre only took women past the halfway point in their pregnancy—and part human decency, because she already knew that Nat didn't have anyone to go to the larger city with her. Or to sit and wait with her.

"Uhm, I guess I thought I would take a cab," the woman said, her voice shaking.

"You don't have anyone you could call? How about the father?"

"He's not...okay, I'll call someone."

Dani felt awful, but it wasn't her place to interject, and Will was waiting for her. But she stepped back anyway and pulled out her notebook, pretending to be busy. "Who will it be? I'll give their name to reception in case you get called back before they arrive."

Nat took a deep breath and Dani felt the prickle of understanding before she heard the next two words. "Jake Foster."

CHAPTER THIRTEEN

Just like that, Dani's memory clicked the pieces together. Long dark hair peeking out of an oversized toque. That Jeep. Nat, short for Natasha. *Probably also goes by Tasha*.

He didn't sleep with her the night of the funeral, she thought desperately. He'd told Dani that, and she'd believed him.

So when did he sleep with her? Nat had said she was still early. It couldn't be Jake's baby.

Curiosity killed the cat, the blood thumping through her veins said. And none of it was her business.

Plus she still had another three hours left in her shift.

"Hey, I thought you'd meet me outside?"

She jerked her head up to find Will standing in front of her with their coffee. "Yeah. Sorry."

"Come on, we're going to get slammed if we're not available again soon."

She nodded numbly and followed along. She checked in with dispatch on auto-pilot, resisting the urge to call Jake and violate patient confidentiality—and girlfriend trust—and ask him what was going on.

But luck was not on her side, because an hour later they were back at Emerg, this time with a toddler who'd had a febrile seizure. A routine call, and he was breathing well, but still in that deep sleep post-seizure that meant they needed to wait and hand-off to the doc directly.

So Dani was standing at the end of the long hallway when the doors slid open and Jake walked in the entrance. And she had a tiny patient, and a patient's panicky, worried mother, to worry about. So she couldn't—wouldn't—read anything like guilt into the stricken look on his face.

He held her gaze for a long, painful moment before introducing himself at the desk. And just then, Will nudged Dani and they were moving into a curtained area and this time it was Dani who gave the report, remembering to look back and forth between the doc and the nurse, double-checking that everything was transcribed to the chart.

And then they were done again, and this time, Dani was *done*. Beyond tired, probably not safe on the job, and emotionally blind-sided. She looked for Jake as they headed through the waiting room, but neither he nor Nat were anywhere in sight. Her phone vibrated in her pocket, and once they were outside, she looked at it.

> **Jake: Come find me when you're done work. Please.**

She couldn't respond, not until she knew more. Tucking her phone away, she sighed and hunkered down into her jacket as they left the overhang at the entrance and headed for their rig again. "Let's see if we can hand this thing off to another team, yeah?"

"JAKE, it's Tasha. I had a car accident and I'm in the hospital in Wiarton. I'm sorry to call..."

"Are you okay?"

"Yeah, I'm fine. But... the thing is...crap. I'm pregnant. And they suggested I call someone..."

Pregnant. The word had thudded into his brain like an anvil.

She'd said some other things, but he'd already been pulling on his clothes and heading for the door.

"I'm on my way." How pregnant?

But he couldn't ask her that on the phone, and now that they were sitting in a curtained off corner of the emergency room, he found he still couldn't form the question.

Tasha looked incredibly awkward, like she regretted calling him. They hadn't exchanged more than a few words in the ten minutes since he'd arrived. His phone vibrated and he looked at it desperately, ignoring the sign above the bed that told him they weren't allowed.

But it wasn't Dani. It was one of her million brothers. He stared at Rafe's name on his screen and he just couldn't swipe into the message. There was too much shit going on for six in the morning that wasn't Dani in his arms.

Jesus. The look on her face—cold, shut-down, all-knowing. If she did know something, she had a one-up on him. And she'd been on the job. *Fuck*. He should have gone over to her. Maybe just said something. Anything.

Instead he sent a lame-ass text, something he promised himself he'd never do again, and now he sat next to another woman. The wrong woman, but he hated how that framed Tasha. She hadn't done anything.

"Hey," he said softly. "Are you sure I can't get you a drink?"

She shook her head. "Listen, Jake…I shouldn't have called you. I know you made it clear before Christmas that we were just a one-time thing. So for me to call you after a couple of months like this…I just panicked."

A couple of months. And she didn't *look* pregnant. But there was only one way to know for sure. “If you’re…I mean…if I’m the…” Wow, brave he was not. “Do you know how far along you are?”

She shook her head. “I have a doctor’s appointment next week, but I’ve been driving back and forth to the city, and my life has been a little crazy.”

A nurse bustled in and introduced herself, then asked a few questions. When she asked about Tasha’s last menstrual period, Jake looked at the floor. She muttered something about maybe December, and he breathed a sigh of relief. “Okay, so maybe you’re about ten weeks along?” The nurse smoothed her hand down Tasha’s arm. “I’m going to do a quick doppler check of your belly then, see if we can hear anything.”

She took a small white machine and a squeeze bottle off a portable cart she’d pulled in behind her. Handing Tasha a large paper towel, she said, “Tuck this in your waistband and scootch your shirt up.”

Jake kept staring at the same scuffed corner of the linoleum, worrying about what Dani was thinking. He wanted the nurse to leave so he could check his phone again, which made him an awful friend. And possibly an awful father. They only slept together once at the beginning of November. Never before had he ever wished so fervently for a partner to have slept with someone else.

A crackle filled the room, then whooshing, and a steady—and fast—little heartbeat. Jake lifted his head, unable to ignore the truth that Tasha was definitely pregnant. Far enough along that there was a strong, healthy baby with a heartbeat in her womb. "Well, that's reassuring, isn't it?" The nurse let Tasha listen for a minute, then cleaned up her belly. "I'm still going to have the doctor come in, but it looks like baby's no worse for wear from the accident."

Jake waited until the nurse left before looking at his friend—and the look on *her* face slayed him in a completely different way. All soft and happy, her relief was obvious. He felt like a jackass for not feeling the same way. Of course he was happy an innocent life could continue to innocently grow, but babies were supposed to be made out of love. *What had he done?*

“It’s probably not yours,” she said quietly.

“Probably?” God, his voice sounded like pure pain.

“We used a condom.”

“And you didn’t with someone else?” *Jesus*, what the *hell* had he been thinking?

He hadn’t been. He’d been grieving and pissed that Dani had him strictly boxed into the friend zone. Two days of sharing a hotel room—even if not at the same time, since they were taking turns at the hospital—and he’d been out of his mind. He’d headed up north to get away from the scent of her on his skin and had tumbled into Tasha’s bed for a single night.

"There's a guy in Toronto. We have a long history."

Jake snorted. He knew something about histories. "I need to tell you that I've got a girlfriend now."

"Shit. I'm sorry."

"No…God, you don't need to be sorry. What we did, we did together." The words sounded strained even to his own ears.

"David—my…whatever he is…—I was with him before you. And again at Christmas. It was…unexpected." He knew something about that, too. "But neither of those timings work out if I…" She shrugged. "I've been trying to make sense of this since I took a test a couple of days ago."

Jake only had the vaguest of understanding of pregnancy dating, but he knew that they weren't going to figure it out between them. "Well, the doctor should be in soon…"

His phone vibrated in his pocket and he snatched it out fast enough his pocket might have started smoking—he didn't look. All he had eyes for was Dani's message.

Dani: I'm done work.
Jake: Don't go home. Wait for me.
Dani: I'm tired.

He wasn't above begging.

Jake: Please, wait. I'll follow you home.
Dani: We can talk later.
Jake: Where are you? I'll come to you now.
Dani: She needs you.
Jake: She needed a friend. That's all.
Dani: Ask her about her paramedics.

Damnit. Dani couldn't come out and say she'd been one of the responders to Tasha's accident, but he could read between the lines. "The ambulance that picked you up. Any chance one of the two paramedics was a pretty brunette named Dani?"

Tasha winced. "Seriously?"

"My girlfriend."

"Small world."

"She saw me come in this morning and she knows we slept together."

"I've screwed things up for you."

No, I did that all on my own. "It's okay."

"You weren't with her when we…"

"No." Not that it mattered. His heart had been, and that he'd risked their future together was inexcusable.

Another text message.

Dani: My brother is looking for you.

Jake flipped over to his other text messages.

Rafe: Widespread power outage in Grey County. All available reservists are on standby in case house-to-house search support is needed if power can't be restored by tomorrow.

Damnit. He tapped back a quick response.

Jake: Roger. Am available. Keep me posted.

"Your phone going to explode?" Tasha tapped his arm. "You can go. I just panicked. I'm fine on my own."

"No one should be alone in the hospital if they've got the option of a friend. Just some work stuff, but it's not urgent." Dani, on the other hand, was urgent. "But I would like to go see my girlfriend for a few minutes."

"Go. The way things sound out there"—she waved beyond the curtain— "makes me think

I'm going to be here for a while. Low priority and all that."

He stood and patted her foot. "Text me if you find out any more before I get back?"

She nodded and he brushed his way through the curtain, not caring that he got a dirty look from the nurse for having his phone in his hand.

DANI SAT in the third floor lounge—a quiet spot few people knew about, particularly at this time of day—and stared at her phone. She'd just finished talking to Tom, who'd filled her in on the call for volunteers. As a park ranger, he worked a reduced schedule in the winter months and could easily take some time off, so he was heading to the armouries now. And knowing Jake's work schedule—and sense of community responsibility—she knew he'd be going to help out as well, because he could.

So when he asked her not to leave town just yet, she agreed. Home was thirty minutes north, and if Jake had his uniform in his truck, he wouldn't need to make the return trip before reporting at the armouries.

No matter how thrown she was by what she'd learned overnight, she wouldn't make him chase her.

And if this was their only chance to connect in the next few days, she wouldn't waste it by being petulant and pouty.

Didn't mean she'd be all sunshine and light, either. His ex-something was pregnant, and he'd been called to the hospital to hold her hand. And he'd *come*. Was he just being a good friend? Or was there more there? Something complicated and heavy and *permanent*?

Jake: Where are you?

She texted him her location and waited. It took an impossibly short and ridiculously long amount of time for him to find her, like time was flexing in all directions as her heart thudded in her chest.

He stepped off the elevator and she watched him looking before he caught sight of her. The slightly wild scan he was doing with his eyes broke her heart a little.

“Over here,” she said, a double dose of deja vu slamming into her. How many times had he come looking for her? She was always his priority, and it was never easy.

“You stayed,” he said roughly, pulling her against him after he crossed the lounge in a few long strides.

“How is…she?”

“Fine. How are you?”

She laughed, short and without humour. “Just a regular night at work.”

"Hardly." He squeezed her tight. "You gotta know…there's a chance it's not mine. We were careful. We used…"

She winced as he trailed off. "Maybe let's not talk about it until you know one way or the other."

"Tell me we're going to be okay, Dani." His voice cracked.

"I'm right here." That was all she could promise him—that they were okay in the here and now. Shaky as fuck, but okay.

"You talk to your brothers? Hear about the power outages?"

She nodded. "I'm going home to sleep for a bit, then I'll probably be working tonight again."

"One of these days, gorgeous…"

"Yeah."

He cupped her cheek, tilting her head back. His thumb traced her cheekbone, a slow and possessive slide that sent shivers all the way to her toes. “I love you. Only you. No matter what.”

Unless a woman that looked a lot like her had his child. That would be a trump card. She knew Jake. They hadn’t talked about it yet, but he was born to be a father. And a family man, nothing part-time about it.

“No,” he said fiercely. “Don’t think that. Whatever just made you shutter yourself like that…If there are consequences to something I did before we were together, I’ll do the right thing. By a *child*. But also by you. Always by you. There’s nothing between Tasha and me.”

Dani closed her eyes. She didn’t want to do this. Didn’t want to feel the wave of panic rising in her chest or the desperate need to hang on to him like he might slip through her grasp.

He swore under his breath. “Damnit. I wish there was a way to undo whatever I’ve done in the past. But she's not…it was never a special thing between us."

His chest shook with emotion as he stormed out the words, and she ached to believe him. No, she *did* believe him, because he didn't look happy to admit that—she knew he hated how that sounded, like something Matt would say. And it was okay…for Matt. And maybe that was part of the problem, that Jake held himself to an impossible standard. God, this was going to be hard no matter what. He didn't need to beat himself up at the same time for something that couldn't be undone. "Okay."

"For real okay?"

She laughed, and this time it felt…stronger. Still surreal, but yes, like they might just be okay.

"You going home now?" His voice dropped to a husky note that made her want to drag him home with her.

She nodded.

"My place." It wasn't a question, really, but she gave another nod. She was *definitely* sleeping in his bed, even if he wasn't in it. He nudged her nose with his, his eyes hot and searching as he brought their faces together. "It's where you belong."

"One thing at a time," she said on a quick breath before he crushed his mouth over hers. It was quick and unsatisfying compared to all the kisses over the last month when they had all the time in the world, but it still lit Dani on fire.

"My place," he repeated with a growl, still holding her face in one of his big, calloused hands. "Never doubt your place in my heart. In my house. In my life."

She took a deep breath. "Call me later." *When you know more.*

"I don't need to report to the armouries just yet. I'll come home for dinner, at least we can have a bit of time after you wake up."

"You don't need to."

"I *want* to. I love you, Dani Minelli. Always have. Always will."

She nodded. He stepped back, and before he could turn and walk away she whispered her own *I love you* to him. He stared at her lips for a final beat before taking a deep breath of his own and heading off.

She did love him. And she trusted that he loved her.

So why did it still feel tenuous, like what they had might still crumble into dust?

CHAPTER FOURTEEN

Another four hours passed before Tasha was seen briefly by an apologetic emergency physician who told them he wasn't qualified to do more than a quick bedside ultrasound to confirm what they already knew from the doppler—baby seemed fine.

At first, he seemed to be suggesting that Tasha just wait to see her family doctor at the scheduled appointment, but Jake wasn't having any of that. He needed to know if he might be this baby's father, and he needed to know as soon as humanly possible.

If he was…well, he'd do the right thing. *However that included Dani*. If she wanted to be included. What a mess. His right eye twitched as he asked if there were any other options.

"We could get you in to the early pregnancy detection unit in Owen Sound tomorrow, probably," the doctor said, scribbling something on an information sheet.

Tasha glanced at Jake and he winced. Owen Sound. At the south end of the peninsula. The opposite direction from her home, and the storm raging outside was only going to get worse. No way could he invite her back to his place, not even if he wanted to, which he didn't. They needed some boundaries. But he could call in a favour.

Twenty minutes later, they swung past the armouries and picked up keys from Corporal Amy Rodgers, who lived in an apartment close by. She wouldn't be sleeping at home tonight, having agreed to be on the stand-by team with

Tom and others. They'd sleep at the armouries, and thankfully, she didn't ask many questions about why Jake had a friend who needed a place to crash. Not in front of Tasha anyway. But once he got Tasha settled with a promise to pick her up in the morning and returned to the armouries for a quick check-in, making sure he could head home and then go to Owen Sound for a medical appointment the next day, Amy was waiting for him. She was a far too clever young woman who knew her rank but also knew how far she could push a senior member, and her teasing grin said it all.

Jake glanced around, making sure they were alone. "Say it, Rodgers. Say it now, and don't say it again."

"Secret girlfriend, Sergeant?"

He sighed. "No. Really not, and it's complicated. You want to help me keep the rumour mill straight?"

"That doesn't sound like any fun at all."

"You want to avoid twenty extras?"

"New Army, you can't do that without cause."

"Smart ass. Tasha is a friend. But I have been seeing someone, and she knows about Tasha but I'd rather her brothers didn't. Or if they do, they know the whole story."

"You've lost me."

"Yeah." He stared through the icy sleet coming down out the window—the freezing rain he was about to drive through like an idiot to hold his girlfriend. The least he could do after that was be honest with the people around them. "This is probably a terrible idea."

"What is?"

"Taking advantage of being locked together in the armouries tonight to lay my cards on the table."

The silence that loomed in his truck the whole way home said it all. It *was* a terrible idea.

He was going to do it anyway.

DANI WOKE up as Jake's arm wrapped around her waist. She held still for a moment, taking her bearings. They were in Jake's room, where she'd fallen asleep as soon as her head hit the pillow. She hadn't heard from him since she'd left the hospital that morning. A part of her *wanted* to close her eyes and go back to sleep. Wanted to hide in slumber instead of dealing with the mess that was her boyfriend crawling into bed without any update on his pregnant ex-girlfriend.

And Dani was too scared to ask for one. But she didn't push him away, either. She needed his arm around her, no matter the mess he brought with his love.

They lay like that until her alarm went off, then they wordlessly got up together.

"I'm going to take a shower," she said, needing a bit of space.

Jake looked like he wanted to join her, and her gut twisted as she ducked his worried gaze and headed for the bathroom alone. “Wait.”

She paused, slowly sliding her head back in his direction.

Apprehension rolled off him in heavy, ugly waves. He looked like he was going to say something else, but opted for safe ground. “Hungry? Grilled cheese?”

“Sure.”

She didn’t wait for the temperature to regulate before she stepped in, needing the sharp prick of cold and then hot against her skin. A reminder she could handle whatever was coming her way, that she didn’t need it easy. As she washed her hair, she thought of Jake, down in the kitchen. He’d been blindsided by this news as much as her, and she’d shut him out.

With a heavy sigh, she towelled off, got dressed, and went to find her boyfriend. *Be supportive*, she told herself. *Even if it kills you*.

He was waiting with a plate of food for them to share, and when he pulled her into his lap at the table, she went with it.

“So we didn’t get any more information about pregnancy dates today,” he said slowly, after they finished eating.

We. She knew he didn’t mean it like that, but her skin crawled at the thought of him having pregnancy related appointments with anyone but her. Shock rippled through her core at that realization. “Oh, that’s too bad.”

A banal response, but better than nothing or worse, harsh words she wouldn’t be able to take back. She squeezed his neck and stood up, busying herself with clearing their plate and glasses of water. So much for being selfless. First hurdle and she’d fallen flat on her face.

"Tasha knows I'm in a relationship. She had an on-again, off-again thing with another guy, and there's a good chance he's the father."

She nodded. He followed her to the sink, wrapping his arms around her waist as she stood there.

"I'm sorry, again."

"You don't have anything to be sorry for," she whispered.

"Want to tell me what you're thinking?"

"Nope."

"Why not?" He kept one arm banded tight around her waist and swept her hair to one side with the other hand, then pressed a kiss to the curve of her neck.

"Because I don't want to be unsupportive. Whatever happens, we'll deal."

Leaning into her a bit, he exhaled slowly. "I like the sound of *we*."

Damn, that made her feel bad for her own reaction to the same word. They stood there, breathing together, on the edge of something either fragile or strong or maybe both, and she couldn't bring herself to say anything. She didn't trust which way the words would go.

"I'm afraid you'll leave me." He took the leap and said the words she'd been afraid to voice herself.

Unexpected tears blurred her vision, and she closed her eyes, refusing to let them fall. "I'm not going to leave *you*. But I'm afraid you'll want to be with your child full-time." *And that would mean being with another woman.*

"In an ideal world, yes. But I only love one woman." He sighed heavily. "This is not the time, but when I think of the future, you're the only person I see by my side. No matter what."

"You say that now, but if that baby is yours, you're going to go to more appointments, and be there when the baby is born, and that will change you." One of the first calls Dani did a ride-along for as a student EMT was a precipitous birth. She'd stood in the corner of the room as the paramedic helped the dad deliver the baby in the bathroom, and the look on that man's face as his child was born would always stay with her.

"Of course it will. But it won't change how I feel about *you*. Nothing has, nothing will."

"Maybe we should just wait and see."

"No. If it turns out not to be my baby, you'll always wonder if I wouldn't have chosen you if things were different."

"Well, then it would be an academic question," she whispered, her words thick and slurred as she tried to talk around the knot in her throat.

"It's not, though. It's a question I can answer now, no matter what happens. I love you now. I will love you forever. I want you to be my partner for life. And if Tasha has my baby, we'll figure out a way to co-parent with her. You and me, and her. But I don't love her. I never have.

We just don't have the kind of connection that makes a marriage work."

He tugged her away from the sink, and they walked hand-in-hand to the couch. Curling up under a blanket together helped. So did Jake's steady breath against her temple.

It took her a long time to work up the courage to say the most pressing point on her mind, and when she did, she just mumbled it into his shirt. He didn't understand her, so she had to clear her throat and start again. "I'd give you up, you know."

"I don't want you to."

"I know. But if you needed to be a full-time dad…I'd understand that." Her voice broke as she said it.

"We'd make it work." He dragged a heavy breath into his chest. "Maybe it wouldn't be that complicated."

She laughed, but it sounded hollow even to her own ears. "Yeah, right."

He didn't answer that, and another thought occurred to her.

It wouldn't be complicated at first. With just one child.

In an instant, she saw what their children would look like. Her dark hair, his ready smile. Dani had spent so long wanting Jake—just a kiss, just a night, just his arms around her—that she'd never allowed herself to fantasize about more. A life together, complete with children and growing old. And now she wanted that more than her next breath. What if one would be enough? To keep it from getting too…complicated.

How to ask him that, so early in their relationship? She burrowed her face deeper into his chest, breathing him in.

"What is it?"

"More of that whole *I'm afraid* stuff."

"You can ask me anything. I promise." He stroked her arm, and she wanted to believe him.

But what if the answer wasn't what she wanted to hear?

It took her another few minutes to work up the courage to ask. "You do want children, right? Not just one?"

He tightened his arms around her. "Yes."

"Would having a child with someone else change that?"

It took him a minute to respond, and when he did it was a single word. "No."

She nodded. "Good."

CHAPTER FIFTEEN

It was amazing what modern medical technology could do—like date a pregnancy with shocking accuracy. Or so promised a pamphlet in the waiting room.

All Jake needed was someone to give him that date, and maybe he'd start breathing properly again.

Jake and Dani had both been let off the hook for work the night before, and had gone to bed early. Together. They hadn't talked any more, but he was holding on to every bit of hope she gave him.

Now he was sitting in an obstetrician's office with Tasha, his heart thudding in his chest.

He'd been up before dawn, and had left Dani in his bed while he went down to the basement and pounded out a hard run on the treadmill. It hadn't done much for his anxiety levels. Then he put coffee on, woke Dani up with a long, slow kiss that helped more than the run did, and finally dragged himself out of the house as the sky started to lighten.

He picked up Tasha from Rodgers' apartment. Their drive to Owen Sound was filled with a lot of silence and small bits of awkward conversation, which was followed by an even more awkward ultrasound once they arrived at the hospital. Tasha had headed in to the ultrasound on her own, but the tech had come back out to the waiting room after fifteen minutes and called out his name. *"I don't want this to be my baby"* seemed like a totally dick thing to say, so he dutifully followed her back to the private exam room where he was shown a healthy baby on a screen, but given zero information. The tech handed Tasha a slip of paper and instructed them to go down the hall to see a doctor.

Thankfully the obstetrician didn't make them wait long. Tasha kept glancing at Jake's bouncing leg, but he couldn't help it. He was nervous.

"Well, Natsaha, you're definitely not ten weeks pregnant. More like somewhere between seventeen to twenty weeks."

"What?" Tasha practically jerked out of her chair, surprise written all over her face. Jake knew how she felt. "Isn't that like...halfway?"

Jake swivelled his head back and forth between the doctor who was still clicking through images on his computer, and Tasha, who was staring at Jake with the same *uhhh, math is hard* look that he felt was painted on his face.

"So what would that make the date of conception?" Jake finally asked, his voice cracking.

The doctor looked at him with a banal look. "That's not a question I get a lot."

Tasha grabbed Jake's hand. "We're just friends. It's complicated."

"I'm getting that. Hang on." The doc lifted a layered cardboard wheel covered in numbers and fiddled with it. "Mid-to-late October."

Relief had never felt so sweet—or so awkward. That timeline leapfrogged right over the only date they'd slept together in November. Jake sagged back in his chair, then twisted to Tasha. "So…"

"Yeah," she gave him a half-hearted grin. "You're off the hook."

Jake looked back at the doctor. "And she's okay?"

"Everything looks fine with the baby. I'll send a note to your family doctor, and write you a requisition for another ultrasound for one week from today. That will give you a more precise date range, and a clear due date."

They left the hospital as they arrived, two people connected in the most tenuous way. Almost friends. One time lovers, but Jake didn't even have a clear memory of what it had been like with Tasha. Dani had crowded that out. He said a small prayer of thanks that this child wasn't his—not that he wouldn't have loved it, but hopefully Tasha had a stronger connection with the father.

Jake waited until they were back on the road to Wiarton before bringing it up. "You should probably talk to him."

"Shut up." The small smile Tasha had been wearing since they left the hospital slipped. "I will."

"If he's not excited, then he's not worthy of you."

Out the corner of his eye, he caught a small frown before she smoothed her expression. "You must really love your girlfriend if you think it's that simple."

A pang of guilt hit Jake square in the chest. "Look, I know not all guys are thrilled about the *idea* of starting a family. My brothers are all like that. But when push comes to shove, a real man steps up. That's all I'm saying."

She lifted her brows in response, but what that meant, he didn't know.

By the time he got Tasha to the garage to pick up her car, which had been given the all clear after a wheel alignment, and made it to the armouries, a group of guys were already back in from a six hour door-to-door search through a local area affected by the power outages. Neighbours were helping each other as much as possible, so it was really just the reclusive characters they needed to worry about, and anyone without phone service.

They were still on standby for a larger rollout, and he was glad he'd gone home the night before. That was the army—hurry up and wait. But not long after he arrived, they got word they were all moving to a community centre closer to the largest blackout area. Jake grabbed his ruck and made sure his section did the same before heading for the buses laid on for them.

The next two days were non-stop work and sleep, with zero privacy. He was able to text with Dani, but he couldn't call her, and that their new relationship was under strain *and* still a secret proved a double challenge that he was ready to be done with.

But his bluster about telling her brothers how he felt couldn't be followed up on until they returned to the armouries, or were back in Pine Harbour. He wasn't sure which he'd prefer. Choosing your poison still mean fucking staring death in the eye and taunting the bastard.

The decision was made for him when they piled on the buses and Rafe announced to a chorus of groans that while they were heading back to the armouries, they weren't quite done just yet—they'd been voluntold to help the Hydro crews the next day, so anyone with the appropriate license was being roped into driving a Hydro truck to free up linemen to do the repair work. One more night of sleeping on an Army cot. As soon as he could hide in a private office, he called Dani and gave her the heads up that he was going to tell Rafe and Tom about them. She laughingly told him he was an idiot, but an idiot she loved, so that just fuelled him up for a battle.

Then he hung up and went to find Tom in the Company Quartermaster office. "Impromptu mess meeting, come on."

Jake waved Rafe over on their way to the back of the building where the Sergeants Mess was located. He had a key to the bar, and it was relatively secluded. Probably no one would hear the yelling.

And if they did, they'd know it was senior NCOs hashing some shit out and mind their own damn business.

"What's going on, Jake?" Rafe turned around in a slow circle, taking in the empty mess.

"Grab a beer."

His friend made a *sure, whatever* face and grabbed three bottles from the fridge.

Opening their bottles at the same time, Tom and Rafe gave Jake matching confused looks.

He set his own bottle down on a table and crossed his arms. "I'm in love with your sister."

Beer sprayed across the empty space between them and Rafe slowly wiped his mouth. "What?"

"And she's in love with me. I thought you should hear it directly."

Tom just sipped his beer, saying nothing. His hooded gaze didn't give anything away, either.

"How…why…" Rafe shook his head. "No, I don't want to know the details. What about that girl up north?"

"Just a friend."

"That you hooked up with after Lynn died." Rafe rolled his shoulder as he spit out the words. "Don't think that the fact I'm still rehabbing this sucker will hold me back from decking you."

"There's no need for that. Dani knows about Tasha."

"Oh yeah? How did that conversation come up?"

"She saw her the night of the funeral. Tasha was at my house when Dani drove me home."

Tom scowled and spoke for the first time. The ice in his voice promised that just because he was the most mild-mannered of the Minellis, he was still a Minelli, and he'd happily fuck Jake up if he deserved it. "That doesn't sound great."

"There's a lot of things that don't sound great. But they're inconsequential."

"Like what?"

It would be better if they knew now. If they took their punches and burned bright now, so when it came up later—and it would, because the entire peninsula had the population of most small towns, and enough people knew he'd been with Tasha that when she was massively pregnant in the spring, tongues would wag.

"Tasha's pregnant." Jake ducked out of the way as Rafe charged. "And it's not mine, asshole."

Rafe whirled and snagged Jake's arm. "You didn't fucking lead with that for no reason. What the hell did you do?"

Jake shoved Rafe hard in the chest. "Back off, man."

"If you've hurt my sister—"

"I said, back off. She might be your sister, but she's *my* Dani. I love her. I don't know—" He cut himself off with a strangled curse. "Nothing gets in the way of that. This other thing…the baby's not mine. But if it was, it wouldn't change anything between Dani and me. She's mine, first and foremost. Nothing touches that."

Rafe scowled at him, then his eyes narrowed. "You love her?"

"I don't ever want to have this conversation again. I don't owe you or anyone else who isn't Dani an explanation about this. But I've loved her for a long time. Now that I have her, I'm not letting her go."

"How long?" His best friend's voice had shifted into exactly the cold, quiet tone he'd always feared.

Jake looked warily between Rafe and Tom, who looked just as murderous as his brother sounded. "We're going to do this once, and you can rail at *me* about that. Leave her out of this."

"How. Long?"

"Long enough that I couldn't do anything about it when I fell for her," he admitted.

Tom exhaled, a long, worrying breath. "Her last summer of high school. You couldn't keep your eyes off her. I thought you'd moved on."

"I did. I knew I had to, so I did, okay? But I've never gotten over her."

"Did you know she had a crush on you?" Rafe scowled. "Did you do something to make that happen?"

"Hell, no." He scrubbed his face. "This was a mistake. We can't have this conversation."

"We should have had it *years* ago, apparently. You were supposed to be like a brother to her. Not break her heart and steal her happiness."

"I haven't—" He broke off. He had no clue how Dani really felt. If this would be too much for her to handle so early in their relationship, and he wouldn't blame her if it was. *One night*. He felt sick at the thought that he might lose her over a foolish night of grief-fuelled escape. "Making her happy is my sole priority, I promise you."

"You're taking a big risk. What happens when you guys break up?" Tom lifted his hands, gesturing at the space around them. "We work together. Live practically on top of each other."

Jake flexed his jaw, then rubbed along it with his knuckles. There was only one way to make Rafe understand, and Tom might not get it at all. Not yet. "Rafe, you went through that with Olivia. Do you regret any of it?"

"Only being stubborn for so long." Still scowling, his best friend since the first grade rocked back on his heels. "It's like that?"

"If you'd gut yourself to give your wife a kidney, then yeah, it's like that."

Tom shook his head. "You're both fucking nuts. One minute Rafe wants to kill you, then you invoke his wife and all of a sudden it's magical flower petals."

His brother shrugged. "Yeah. You'll understand one day."

DANI WORKED ONCE while Jake was gone, but each night she ended up staying at his house instead of going home. Her parents hadn't asked where she was staying, although it wouldn't take long for Rafe and Tom to share the news.

She didn't care if she was taking the weenie way out. She wasn't up for any more drama, and didn't want anyone's opinion about her and Jake's relationship.

Not that hiding was doing her any good, either. Really, the last thing she needed was time in a big, empty house to think about the near-miss natural consequences of Jake sleeping with another woman. It didn't matter how enlightened or understanding Dani was *supposed* to be. In reality, when left to the quiet echo of her innermost thoughts, she burned with jealousy.

At something that ended up being nothing.

But it niggled, nonetheless.

That he'd gone to another woman after Lynn died, after he lost the closest person to a sister he'd ever had. Found comfort in another pair of arms. Inside her body.

It should have been enough that Dani was in Jake's bed now, that his house smelled like her enough that when he got mad he had to leave. That should have made her giggle and clap her hands together. They were finally as they should be—Jake+Dani. Forever.

It was too bad they hadn't had the time to sink into a forever type of relationship, one with a foundation strong enough to weather storms like this.

As if Jake was right next to her, curled up against her back, she felt his breath against her ear. *You don't think we have a strong foundation?* They would. But the concrete was still curing, for heaven's sake. *I'm the contractor, gorgeous. You let me worry about whether or not we're up to code*.

He was good like that. He'd waited. She'd been ready to throw herself at him while still in college, damn the consequences. And he'd pushed her away…so she'd come home with a boyfriend.

She rolled over, grabbing her phone. She'd set it on his side of the bed the night before. The clock blinked silently at her. Quarter to six. He'd be up, wherever he was.

> **Dani: Did you go to Afghanistan because I came home with a boyfriend?**

It didn't take him long.

Jake: Good morning.
Dani: Answer me. It's important.
Jake: What are you doing?
Dani: Testing how old some concrete is.
Jake: I don't understand, but okay. Uhhh, yes. In part.

Honest to a fault, that was Jake. Tears slipped sidewise down her face, splashing over her nose onto the pillow and wetting her cheek.

Dani: Sometimes it's hard for me to remember that this isn't exactly new between us.
Jake: Just think of how hard it was for me to remember that we weren't together. That I didn't have a right to punch all those guys in the face for touching you.

She smiled through her sniffles.

Dani: What did I interrupt with my

crazy demands?
Jake: Hay box breakfast. We're about to roll out and provide support to the electrical company.
Dani: K. Stay warm.
Jake: You gotta know...I don't regret going. It's my job, and it's important. You being with someone else made the timing right. But you didn't send me fleeing the county, okay?

How could she respond to that? Nothing seemed significant enough, so after a minute she just typed a quick **I<3U**, watched the keystrokes turn into an animated heart on her phone, as if it was just that easy, then buried her face in his pillow. The tears would dry by the time he got home. He'd never know how much of a mess she was.

When she woke up the second time, she didn't even look at her phone. If Jake was out in the freezing cold helping senior citizens, she could at least do some laundry. That led to pulling a roast out of the freezer, which inspired her to make muffins.

Except Jake didn't have any baking powder. Or baking soda. Or brown sugar. In fact, given his pantry, the only thing she probably could make would be plain tea biscuits, and that would use up the last of his butter.

She debated calling her mother. *"So, yeah, that boyfriend? It's Jake. And I need baking supplies. Mind sending Dad down the road in his four-wheel-drive?"*

The muffins could wait. Maybe she'd let her brothers tell her parents and just hide out here until she needed her summer clothes.

As if on cue, her phone rang. A brother this time, not a mother.

"Zander, to what do I owe the—"

"Seriously, you're dating Jake Foster?"

"Seriously. I know, it's like, oh my god, right? When did you turn into a teenage girl?"

"Do you know how many women he's— "

She cut him off again, because *no*, not exactly, and for the sake of her sanity, that knowledge was going to remain unknown. "Let's start again. Hey, big brother, what's up in the Arctic tundra?"

"Bet you have more snow than we do."

"Bet that lie you guys tell yourselves about it being a *dry cold* really bites this time of year."

Zander laughed in her ear. "You okay?"

"I'm at his house right now, thinking about making muffins. I'm fine. You talked to Rafe and Tom?"

"On speaker phone this morning. They followed Jake around for a minute while I gave him a piece of my mind."

Dani muffled a laugh.

"He seems serious."

"I know." It was overwhelming. "It's lovely."

"You're making muffins for him?"

"Not really. He doesn't have all the ingredients, so I was going to do some online shopping instead. He wants to take me to the regimental ball."

Zander made a listening type noise that meant he'd come, said his peace, and now he would mumble along in the background until she tired of talking at him.

"So I might get a dress. And some lingerie."

Or until he proved less mature than her and begged for mercy.

She laughed as he said a quick good-bye.

The lingerie had just been a threat to get Zander off her back. The truth was, Jake preferred her naked. She blushed as she remembered how quickly he liked to get every last layer off her body. But a dress…

She opened her laptop and surfed through a few websites before stumbling on the perfect dress. Dark red, strapless, fitted to the hips then long layers of tulle making an ethereal skirt. Her heart skipped a beat until she saw the price. *Never going to happen.* She sagged against the table. No fantasy was worth half her paycheque. Olivia would understand.

Her sister-in-law picked up on the first ring. "Want to come over and make cookies?"

Dani laughed. "No. I had a fleeting moment of almost making muffins, but it passed." She hesitated. "And I'm at Jake's, so I'd have to drive into town and I don't think the salt trucks have been down the road yet."

"Yeah…about that. When were you going to tell me?" Olivia was teasing, her tone was clear and sparkly, but Dani still felt guilty.

"It's complicated."

"So I hear. But all's well that ends well?"

"Yes…" Dani told her about her dress plan and how badly they needed a night out—a formal coming out as a couple, something magical to reconnect.

"I think you're underestimating the connection you guys have, but why not go for it? It sounds gorgeous, maybe you can wear it again."

"The fact that I *never* wear fancy dresses is exactly why I need to buy one now. I didn't even wear something this fancy for your wedding. Hell, I might not to my *own* wedding."

Peals of laughter filled her ear. "If you think Jake's going to have anything less than a black tie wedding complete with a five-piece band when he puts a ring on your finger, you're out to lunch."

When he puts a ring... Prickly awareness skittered across her skin. Of course she knew in the abstract that was a possibility—there wasn't anything halfway about Jake, or how they felt about each other. And he was definitely at that point in his life. She was sitting in the middle of a forever family home, for goodness sake. But if Olivia could see that as plain as day…and here Dani was just sitting worrying about a *date*. Now she had to worry about something so much bigger. And scarier, because she was pretty sure she wanted to put a ring on *his* finger, too.

"You there, honey?"

"Uh…yep."

"Did I freak you out?"

"Little bit."

"First things first. Let's find you a knock-off version of that dress…"

Maybe it was a bit of a Cinderella game, but they could use a fairytale night of romance.

Then everything could return to normal. Or not. Maybe Dani's idea of normal was long gone.

CHAPTER SIXTEEN

Restless was a definite understatement for how Jake felt. Dani had kicked him out of the house mid-afternoon so she could get ready for the Valentine's Day Regimental Ball. He had an important stop to make, but first he wanted to be in uniform. And before that, he was long overdue for another visit at the Howard house.

Gavin and Jack were playing ball hockey when he pulled up. He grabbed a stick and joined in, only stopping when their dad stuck his head out and called them in to do their homework.

“Gavin’s getting quick with the stick out there,” Jake commented as they all stripped off their outerwear in the kitchen.

Ryan nodded. “Thinking of putting him in some camps this summer.”

“Yeah?” That was a huge step, but Jake didn’t call attention to it.

“And I’m going to dance camp,” Maya announced, balancing on top of a chair. “To be a ballerina.”

“I bet you are.” In the last few months, the tiny blonde whirlwind had sprouted, and now she looked like a prettier version of her brothers. No more baby left in her. He glanced at Ryan, who just picked his daughter up. She wrapped her arms around his neck and snuggled close. Well, maybe not totally grown up. “How old are you now, Maya? Seven?”

She giggled.

“Ten?” Jake scratched his chin when she peeked back at him. “Ninety-five?”

She shook her head and held out four fingers. “Almost four.”

“Wow. I hear that’s the best age ever.”

A nod. “And I’ll have a cake.”

“Are you having a party?”

Nodding again, she wiggled her legs. Ryan understood the unasked request and set her down again. “You can come to my party.”

“Okay.”

“It’s for ballerinas.”

Ryan snorted. “We’ll have to make Jake a special tutu. He probably doesn’t have one.”

“I’d wear one for Maya.”

She dashed off, followed by her brothers who were making rude comments about farting on tutus, but Ryan just ignored them. “I’m going to hold you to that, by the way.”

“I’ll come to her party.”

"I meant the tutu wearing part."

Jake shrugged. There were worse things in the world than a bit of tulle and ribbon.

"So you and Dani, huh?"

He couldn't hold back a grin. "Yep."

"How long has that been going on?"

"Christmas."

Ryan nodded. "Good. You making her happy?"

"I'm trying. I bought her a ring."

"Holy shit. She say yes?"

"Haven't asked her yet." But she would. There was so much love between them it was ridiculous.

"You guys have gotten over that drama with your girl from Tobermory, eh?"

Jake bristled. "Tasha wasn't my girl."

"Sorry."

He waved it off. “Nah, my own fault. So you heard about that. Great.”

Ryan laughed. “Sorry, again. Nothing escapes the Pine Harbour grapevine.”

“Including that you’re not going back to work. Dani said you’ve given your notice.”

Ryan scrubbed his palm up across his jaw. “The end of my leave of absence is coming up and I just can’t be away from my kids thirty-six hours a week right now.”

“Hey, no judgement from me. You want to pick up some school-time work from me? I can always use another set of strong arms.”

“Nah, I’m good. We don’t need much, and I’m coming back to the unit for weekly parade. Going to be an Army bum for a bit. Olivia’s agreed to watch the kids on parade nights, and it’ll keep me shaving at least once a week, anyway. Plus there’s the movie people…they’ll be showing up in a month.”

"The Fenichs leave you holding the ball on that?" The film stars were going to be staying in the cottages Jake had helped build up and down Jake's lane, heading toward the lake. It had been something Gloria and Lynn had been excited about. Jake had forgotten about it since the funeral.

"I don't mind. They're tenants like anyone else."

Ryan was the least star-struck person Jake knew—which made him a perfect go-to guy should any of them have problems with their accommodations. "You know you can call me if something needs fixing?"

His friend laughed. "You know I know how to use a hammer, right?"

"Wouldn't have offered you a job if you didn't."

It was tempting to just sit there and pretend all was fine and ordinary. Like Ryan's wife hadn't been murdered a few months earlier. But Jake didn't think doing that would make him a good friend. So even though he knew it wouldn't go over well, he opened the can of worms. "You still seeing a counsellor?"

"Yeah." No additional information offered.

"The kids?"

"No...they didn't like it. We'll try again in a month or two."

"You liking it?"

"Not even a little bit." He let out a heavy sigh. "If I didn't have so much trouble leaving the kids with other people, I wouldn't go at all. But I know I need to get over that. So...there you go."

"I wasn't digging." Jake rocked back on his chair. "We could babysit, too."

"Yeah...Dani offered."

"We love the kids." *And you, you big lug*, but he didn't add that. "Keep us in mind."

"Will. Now don't you have to go climb into an uncomfortable uniform?"

Jake laughed. "Nice. Get me to promise to wear a tutu, then kick me out of your house."

"You going to ask Dani to marry you tonight?"

"Think so, yep."

"Then yeah, I'm kicking you out. Get to it." Ryan stood and offered his hand, wishing him luck.

Since Jake was headed to Dani's parents' house next, he'd need it.

A quick pit stop at Dean's place to get into his uniform—and get one last pep talk from his bachelor-for-life older brother, which he didn't really listen to—and then he found himself walking up the steps of the Minelli home. It was damn cold, but one didn't wear a parka over a dress uniform, no matter what. He knocked, then stood tall, as if good posture might ease the nervous ache in his gut. It didn't.

"Jake, what a surprise," Anne Minelli said dryly. They hadn't actually seen each other since Dani had confirmed for her parents that they were dating, although she'd promised the conversation had been easy and uneventful.

"I hope it's okay that I dropped in."

"Of course." Anne was still wearing the catering company branded shirt that Jake was quite familiar with. Dani wore the same shirt every summer for years as she worked for her mother throughout high school and college.

"You just get off work, or are you heading out?"

"I have a dinner I'm catering tonight, but there's lots of time before I need to leave. I understand you and Dani are heading to the armouries tonight for a fancy do."

"We are. Is Alessandro around?"

Awareness dawned in her eyes. "Ah. Yes, he's in the back room, reading. Why don't you wait in the sitting room?"

He nodded curtly and headed for the formal living room at the front of the house. No television, uncomfortable furniture. No fun.

“So, a soldier has come calling, eh?” Dani’s father’s voice rumbled behind him, and Jake spun.

“Yes, sir.”

“Sit.” It was an order. Jake sat, carefully perching on the edge of an occasional chair. Alessandro Minelli—businessman, father, immigrant, and complete enigma—sat across the room on the sofa. Anne poured them each a drink of scotch, then sat beside her husband.

“I understand that Dani told you we’ve fallen in love,” Jake started, but that was as far as he got.

“She did. And then my sons reported that after you started taking up with my daughter—my only daughter, my baby, the light of my life—

that you found out an ex-girlfriend was pregnant."

Jake nodded, keeping his cool. No way would Rafe and Tom tell their father that and not share the entire story. He wouldn't have made it in the door if they had. So this was a test, one he intended to pass with flying colours. "I did, but as I hope you're aware, sir, the child wasn't mine. And if it had been, that wouldn't change anything."

The older man grunted. "That doesn't impress me much."

"There are some conversations that aren't meant to take place between generations, sir."

"Such as?"

"Such as the details of former relationships. Or current ones. But I'd like to reassure you that my relationship with that other woman was brief, and ended long before Dani and I started seeing each other." Jake took a deep breath, then leaned forward, looking Dani's parents in the eye with earnest intent. “I love your daughter. Very much. She is the only woman I have eyes for—and will have eyes for, for the rest of my life.”

“Is that what you came here for? To reassure us of your affection for Daniella?” Anne asked softly.

“No.” *Brave and bold, man.* ”I’m going to ask Dani to marry me. And I’d like to tell her I have your blessing when I do.”

Two blank faces stared back at him for the world’s longest minute. But he hadn’t grown up one of four boys without learning a thing or two about staring contests.

Finally Anne sighed and looked down at her hands. “This is going to come out wrong, so bear with me. I know that I can be a bit…fierce when it comes to my children. But you need to understand that marriage is—or at least it should be—a permanent decision. Building a life with someone shouldn’t be done because of an infatuation.”

"I'm not…this is not an infatuation." He said the words slowly and carefully, not wanting to leave any room for doubt. "I love everything about Dani. Her heart, her generous spirit, her sense of loyalty and how much she values her family. Her skill as an EMT and the steady way she powers through almost any adversity. The way she laughs. That she likes to sleep in and hates to do dishes. I think about my life five or ten years down the road and she's by my side. I want her to be the mother of my children. This is not an infatuation."

"For you." Anne shook her head. "I believe it's not for *you*."

No. He wasn't on his own at the edge of this cliff. "I believe Dani loves me too."

"And it's her question to answer, not ours," her father said gruffly. "But you've only been dating a very short time. Other than when she was at college, she's always lived with us. And now she's staying with you? Without any time on her own? Without a normal build-up toward a serious relationship?"

Anne took her husband's hand and sighed. "Rafe and Olivia struggled so much when they rushed into their marriage. They were the same age as Dani. Maybe you don't see that because you're..." She trailed off and shrugged. "We love you, Jake. And we hope you two are very happy together. But don't rush into something because it's new and exciting."

Shit. "I will take that under advisement."

Dani's father laughed, and it wasn't without mirth. Jake blinked at him, and he waved his hand. "If you do, it'll be a first for us. You'll understand when you're a parent...offering advice usually is an exercise in futility."

JAKE HAD SAID he'd be back to pick her up at six. Dani was pacing back and forth in his room—their room, for all intents and purposes—at quarter to the hour. She'd had a long bath and shaved her legs—and a bit more, because hey, it was Valentine's Day—then practically rolled around in moisturizing lotion because it was winter. She'd paid careful attention to her makeup—sleek and dark—and her hair—up and sexy. And she was still done early. The whole girly routine wasn't for her. Except for the part where she felt like a million bucks—she liked that part.

He'd told her that he'd take care of her jewelry, and Olivia had disclosed that she'd been pumped for details about Dani's dress neckline, so she trusted he'd put thought into that. Which made her ready to go…she just needed a soldier to go with.

Right on command, the front door opened. She grabbed her heels off the bed and scampered to the landing at the top of the stairs.

“Over here,” she said with a little laugh, loving the way his eyes lit up as he took in her dress. The skirt swirled around her legs as she descended and the whole world narrowed to the space between them.

“You take my breath away,” he said quietly. “I’m not sure I want to share you with anyone.”

She knew the feeling. “I’m all yours.”

He carefully eased against her, cupping her face as he kissed her softly. She pressed into him, loving how he barely moved, even as she wound her arms around his neck and gave herself into the kiss. But he wasn’t unaffected—his hands roved over her as the rest of him held stock-still. He skimmed her breasts, her hips, her bottom, tugging her closer with each caress, and for a minute, she thought he really might just take her upstairs. He seemed hungrier than usual for her tonight, his grip a little more possessive—not that she was complaining. “I’m going to look forward to unwrapping you at the end of the night.”

"Me, too."

He held her gaze with a long, heated, and surprising heavy look of his own for a moment before pulling back. "Time for your promised bling."

She followed him into his office, where he hesitated beside his desk for a moment before pulling open a drawer.

The jewellery box he pulled out was long and slim, and for a moment she had a flash of him holding a smaller, square box instead. Ever since Olivia had put that image in her head, she'd been turning over in her head what kind of wedding she'd like. What kind of *marriage* she'd like, because if her brother's experience had taught her anything, it was that the wedding was just the start. The easy part, for all the fuss and bother.

But she understood Olivia's point too, that Jake would want that fuss and bother because he'd had to keep his feelings to himself for so long.

She wanted to show him she was ready to be his partner in life, however he needed to her be, be it an evening of her on his arm, or when the time was right, throwing the biggest, glitziest wedding Pine Harbour would ever see.

With trembling fingers she lifted the delicate necklace off its velvet bed. Small bezel set rubies and diamonds dotted the thin gold chain. She fumbled at the clasp, then gave up, just holding it in her hand as she held it up. Jake's office was lit with pot lights and a desk lamp, and the light from all different directions seemed to bounce off the tiny gems, making the whole thing sparkle in the prettiest way.

"I thought it would match your dress," he said, moving around her body, his hand trailing across her hip and up her back. When his fingers hit the bare skin at the top of her dress, she shivered.

"Olivia gave up the colour, too?"

"I was persuasive."

"What did you say?"

"Never you mind." He kissed her shoulder, then her neck, before bringing his lips to the curve of her ear. "I thought it would match you naked, too."

She shuddered and tipped her head to the side, baring her neck to him.

"Your ears look bare." He mock sighed, and she smiled to herself. She was being spoiled tonight.

"I didn't get you anything."

"You have no idea how much you've given me, Dani." He pulled a matching pair of earrings from his pocket, and she put them on as he did up the necklace around her neck. Each brush of his fingertips—against her collarbone, the side of her neck, then lingering at her nape even after he'd secured the clasp—felt electric and special.

She turned slowly, bringing her hands to his chest. She traced his service medals, then brought her hand to his face, giving him back some of the magic he'd just stirred in her. "I've never thanked you for kissing me that night at the Hedgehog."

"Pretty sure it wasn't a favour, gorgeous." He thumbed her lower lip, now completely devoid of lipstick. She couldn't care less. "Did I thank you for coming over the next morning and rocking my world?"

She laughed. "Again…not a selfless act."

"Well, then let's go to a ball, and be thankful together." He offered her his arm and pointed for the door.

CHAPTER SEVENTEEN

By ten o'clock, Jake was more than ready to leave. His girlfriend, on the other hand, was the belle of the ball—literally.

Dani was radiant as she moved around the room, either on her own or on his arm. She disarmed officers and made junior enlisted men blush, and the entire time made sure Jake knew he was the centre of her world. He shouldn't have chickened out earlier. He'd been so close to getting down on one knee, but he couldn't get the warning from her parents out of his head. There would be another opportunity. Dani would be just as happy with a proposal during breakfast in bed as on V-Day.

And Jake didn't want to ignore the possibility that he was more ready to move on to the next stage of their relationship than she was. He knew they'd need to talk about it at some point.

He didn't think it would be on the drive home.

She sat curled up on the passenger side of his truck, wrapped in a heavy wool pashmina with his parka draped over her lap, because it was minus five and even though he'd heated up the truck first, her dress was just layers of nothing. Lovely nothing, but not warm at all. And at first she talked about the evening, and dancing, and he was listening—really—but he was also paying attention to the road. So he almost missed the moment when Dani proved he didn't need to worry.

"Which is more your speed? The ball tonight or what Rafe and Olivia did on New Year's Eve?"

"Both were fine."

"Fine?" Her teasing tone grabbed his attention and he slid a quick glance away from the road. "No preference?"

"Well, tonight is an annual thing. I don't think your mother can handle Rafe getting married again, so that was probably a one-time only event."

"Jake." The way she said his name, low and slow and full of heat, made him look at her all over again. And this time, he saw she wasn't just teasing, but saying a lot more than the words coming out of her mouth.

"Oh."

She grinned and he took her hand before returning most of his attention to the road.

"Well, I'd like a bigger wedding than what Rafe did."

"Mmm hmmm."

"And maybe not in the winter." He rubbed his thumb across her knuckles. "Whatever dress you wear, I'd rather it not be covered up by my coat."

"Agreed."

"Maybe rent a big tent and have it at the house?" She made a noncommittal hum and he squeezed her hand. "How about you? What's your speed?"

"Cottage barbecue, vows on a dock, like at the Fenichs' place." She said it quickly, then gasped at herself like she'd surprised herself with the quick and ready answer.

He laughed. "Didn't know that about yourself?"

"Nope."

"Okay, good to know."

"Good to know? Not, okay, that's what would we do?"

A smirk tugged at the corners of his mouth against his better judgement.

"Wow." She laughed and wiggled her fingers inside his hand. "Fine. It's not like these are imminent decisions. I've got time to wear you down."

"You know…usually before a couple starts talking about weddings, the guy asks the girl an important question."

She didn't have a quick retort for that, and he had a couple of turns to make off the highway and through town, so he didn't notice her twisting in her seat until her foot slid into his lap. Her bare foot, attached to her bare leg. His dick knew what he'd find before he turned his head fully and found his gorgeous woman leaning back against the passenger door, her skirt hiked high on her spread thighs. And her hand was the only thing obscuring whether or not she was still wearing her panties. “You sure I can’t convince you my way is best?”

A chuckle rumbled through his chest. Hell, she could talk him into getting married in clown suits if this was her negotiating stance. “This turning you on?”

She nodded and rocked against her hand, her leg sliding under his touch as she shifted. “I’m so wet.”

Jesus. He’d drive off the road if he wasn’t careful. “I bet.”

“Want to touch me?”

“When we get home, absolutely.”

She groaned, an almost silent noise that worked its way under his skin in zero seconds flat. “Your fingers feel so much better than mine.”

“Two minutes.”

“I can probably make myself come in less than that.”

"Don't." He squeezed her foot and pulled it against the erection straining at the thick fabric of his dress uniform pants. "Ninety seconds."

"You can't rip my dress." She slowly smoothed the tulle down her legs.

Jake rocked his hips against her foot. "You can't rip my uniform."

"Are you really going to ask me—"

"Shhhh. Be a good girl and do as you're told." He tapped the garage door remote as he slid in the driveway at home, pulling into his spot. On the other side of the garage, Dani's car sat exactly where it belonged. "Upstairs. Your choice how the dress comes off."

He was out of the truck and around to her side by the time she had her shoes and wrap all gathered up, and she let him pick her up, which was for the best. He was carrying her upstairs whether she liked it or not. In their room, he set her down, then started taking off his uniform, draping the jacket, then the tie and shirt, over the chair in the corner. Dani just stood in the middle of the room, barefoot with her arms twisted behind her back, her hair tumbling loose from the updo she'd styled it into earlier. In her dark red dress she looked like a fallen angel, all shadows and sin.

He paused and just looked at her for a minute, then pulled out his phone and randomly selected some music. Anything to push out the nagging doubt in the back of his head that he should drop to his knees now and beg her never to change her mind. Beg her to always want him as much as she did tonight.

But she deserved more than begging. She deserved promises and trust.

He docked his phone on the speakers on his dresser, classic Nine Inch Nails quietly swirling around them, and he paced toward her. He was still wearing his pants, but it was her turn to strip. He gestured slowly with his index finger for her to turn around. She bit her lower lip and fluttered her eye lashes low on her cheeks as she did as instructed.

“You’re so damn saucy, Dani. What did I do to deserve you?” He kissed the base of her neck, right below the necklace he’d given her.

“You waited,” she whispered as he unzipped the back of her dress. She grabbed the fabric as it slipped off her torso and he resisted the urge to haul her backwards against him until after she tucked her dress onto the chair on her side of the bed.

But when she glided toward him, wearing just the skimpiest, laciest pair of panties he’d ever seen on her, he let his restraint fall away. Two rough jerks and his pants were undone. Two big steps and they were falling together onto the bed, mouths colliding and hands groping everywhere.

And she was just as wet as she’d promised in the truck.

JAKE SLID her underwear to the side, hissing when he found her wet and bare, swollen and ready.

"Inside me," Dani begged, and he thrust his fingers deep, stretching her as he moved over her. "Jake…"

"I love the way you say my name when you're turned on."

"I love the way you get me off when I'm turned on."

"So feisty tonight." He nipped at her lower lip, then sucked it into his mouth. She felt the soft tug all the way through her body, and it made her nipples ache and her clit pulse. From a kiss.

"You started it by not letting me have my fun in the truck."

He loomed over her, eyes glittering and mouth wet from their kisses. "That was a matter of safety."

"Such a protector," she whispered, arching into his slow and steady touch.

"Never gonna apologize for that. You're precious to me." He kissed his way to her breasts, sucking first one nipple into his mouth, then the other. That drove her out of her mind, and she bucked off the bed, wanting more of him. He yanked her underwear down her hips as he moved quickly down her body, then kissed her mound before latching on to her entire sex with his hungry, eager mouth.

Liquid heat flooded her legs, then poured into her abdomen. Dani cupped her breasts and bit her lip, still feeling the tug of his mouth in all the places he'd sucked on his way to her clit. Worth the wait, and so much better than her fingers. He wasn't the only one who was rewarded for waiting. He slid his hands under her hips, holding her sex right where he wanted as he licked her straight to a first earth-shattering orgasm. First of many he wanted to give her, she guessed through a muzzy haze as he slowly kissed first one thigh, than the other, waiting for her to come down from sensory overload. But he didn't move, and before she could tell him to get his ass up the bed and fuck her already, he was between her folds again, driving her back over the edge.

This time, he didn't wait for her to come down before surging up and into her body, his thighs pushing hers wide as he gripped his erection in one hand and braced himself over her with the other, rocking into her as he did what was essentially a one-armed push-up.

She'd have been more impressed by that if she wasn't entirely distracted by the feeling of being joined as one with the man she loved. Pure, orgasmic bliss. She'd never get enough of that stretch as he filled her, hard and hot and wanting. Never stop craving him on top of her, claiming her as his own.

And it was a claiming, a possessive fuck made all the more intense because of how beautiful he was—all sculpted muscles and bright eyes, whispered words and hungry hands. He'd wound himself around her, one hand splayed wide in the middle of her back as he moved them as one, thrusting his hips hard against hers, the other palming a breast in a clear statement. *Mine*.

She wasn't sure if she orgasmed a third time or if the second one just hadn't ended when he joined her, spilling himself deep on a final jerk. Either way, she was limp and sated, a woman thoroughly loved on every level. As if she didn't know already, he muttered it against her hair, then her neck, and finally her mouth. "Love you so much. More than I can say."

"I know," she whispered after he kissed her deeply, his tongue still hungry, as if they hadn't just made the kind of intense love that they usually fell asleep from.

Inside her, he thickened just enough to let her know he wasn't done, and she half-laughed, half-groaned. "More?"

"More," he grinned, recovering quickly.

"In the shower, then," she said, slapping his chest. "Because I love you."

"And not because you love orgasms?"

"There's a tipping point where the high isn't worth the soreness."

He froze over her. "You're sore?"

She shook her head. "Not yet." And even if she was, she didn't want this night to end. It felt like they'd added a new layer of connection, something deep and thick and wonderful, and she wanted to luxuriate in it. Even if she'd ache the next day.

"I'll have to be gentle, then, just in case."

"Not too gentle," she whispered as he kissed between her breasts, plumping them together for his mouth.

"So gentle. Just my fingers. Slowly, ever so slowly. I love how wet you get when I pet you like that. You squirm so hard against me, and your skin turns the prettiest shade of pink."

She groaned, tipping her had back as her sex bloomed again, ready for him like she hadn't just *had* him. "Screw that, and screw the shower."

"Nuh-uh-uh." He dragged himself off the bed, keeping his hands on her until all he touched was her foot, and then he tugged on her leg until she joined him on shaky legs. "Gentle. I've got my orders."

"Belay that order."

"Too late. My queen has spoken. Whisper soft touches."

"I'm going to kill you."

"May I suggest a tongue-lashing?"

With a laugh, Dani gave him a feeble shove. Oh, he'd get a tongue-lashing. It wasn't like she could stand anyway. Might as well do something on her knees.

DANI FELL ASLEEP AS SOON as their heads hit their pillows again. Jake held her close, a million thoughts racing through his head. He probably wouldn't have heard his phone ring if it hadn't been playing music softly in the otherwise silent room. When the music cut out and the screen flashed to a name he could read from across the room, he was tempted to let it go. It was middle of the night on a Friday, and there weren't any Army exercises going on. But it could be one of his guys—either from the unit or an employee—and if there'd been an accident and he'd ignored it, he'd never forgive himself.

But when he padded across the room, it wasn't a name he wanted to see on the screen.

"Hello?" He poured as much *keep this short* crispness as he could into that single word.

"Jake?" Tasha's voice slipped hesitantly into his ear, like she knew she maybe shouldn't be calling him at quarter to one in the morning.

"What's wrong?"

"Nothing. I'm fine."

He looked back at Dani, still sleeping in his bed. Their bed. He grabbed a pair of sweats—because he didn't need to be naked for this conversation—and stepped out into the hall. "It's the middle of the night."

"I'm in Port Elgin at my sister's, and I'm driving home tomorrow. Thought maybe we could have breakfast."

"I've got plans." Breakfast in bed plans with someone who wouldn't like this phone call, he knew that in his gut.

"I talked to David. He's not thrilled. About the baby."

"I'm sorry to hear that." He really was, that was a shitty turn for her. "I can't be a stop on your way north and south anymore, Tash."

It took her a minute to say anything, and when she did, her voice was small and sad. “You were so good, in the hospital.”

He cut her off, because there weren’t any buts to that sentence. He had a girlfriend, full stop. “You shouldn’t have called me tonight. Or in general. I mean, if you were in a real bind or something…no. There have to be other people in your life that you can turn to, people you haven’t slept with.”

“I thought we were friends.”

“Well, I thought so too, but this conversation has me thinking otherwise.”

“Oh.”

He sighed. “I wish you well, I really do. But you can’t call me in the middle of the night, okay?”

“Shit.“ She started to cry, and he ground his teeth together.

“Can you talk to your sister?”

Wavering breaths filled his ear for a minute, then she sniffed and cleared her throat. "Yeah. I just…I don't want anyone else to know how much I've fucked up, ya know?"

"Jesus, Natasha. You haven't fucked up."

"It doesn't feel like that from here. I didn't even know I was like five months pregnant. What the hell kind of mother am I going to make?"

He laughed. "Probably an average one. No, a great one. Listen, go wake up your sister and tell her all of this. She's going to be a better support to you than I can be."

"God, how much do I suck that I needed to have someone else tell me that?" She groaned. "Okay. Sorry for waking you up."

He didn't bother to correct her, and just waited for her to disconnect the line.

"Jake?" For the second time in as many minutes, a woman said his name like a question. But the specifics of that question —*Can I trust you? Are you my knight in shining armour?*—were different coming from Dani. He'd welcome them from her, though, and wished they didn't go unasked.

"I didn't realize you were still awake."

"I woke up when you left the room." *To take her call*. She didn't say the second part of the statement out loud, but it might as well have been lit up on the wall in neon writing.

"I only stepped out because I thought you were asleep. I didn't want to wake you. It was Natasha." He used her full name, suddenly guilty for being so familiar with her for so long when distance would have been healthier for them all.

"I heard."

"Did you hear me tell her that we don't have a relationship? That I wish her well, but I can't be someone that she leans on?"

"I did."

"She wants to have breakfast tomorrow. I told her no."

"Why?"

"Because the only person I want to have breakfast with is you."

Even in the mostly dark room, he could make out a smile. "I appreciate that. But I meant, why does she want to have breakfast?"

"I don't know." And any guesses weren't ones he'd voice to Dani.

She sighed. "If she asked you after you told her you couldn't be a support person for her, then maybe she has a good reason."

"Or maybe she's alone and that sucks."

"I'm going to regret saying this, but if that's the case…maybe you *should* be a friend to her."

He shook his head. "Not if it interferes with our relationship. She can find other friends."

"That's…cold."

"It's not. She has a sister. I know she has friends in Tobermory, too. She just hasn't told any of them about the pregnancy yet. She will, and it'll all work out. Now let me back into bed."

She lifted the covers for him, then curled into his side with a yawn. "I sleep so much better with you than without you."

"What do you say we make that an official thing? You sleeping here every night?"

Her fingers, which had been lazily sliding through the hair on his stomach, froze in mid-stroke. After their conversation in the truck—and the mind-blowing sex—Jake was pretty sure they were on the same track, so he just waited. "That's not scary for you?" she asked quietly.

He shook his head. "I'm done living without you. No reason for you to keep any of your clothes at your parents' place."

"It's not just clothes," she mumbled into his chest. "I've got a doll collection and an antique sewing machine, plus the acres of paisley fabric I always wanted to make into flouncy curtains."

That didn't sound like… "Is this a weird middle of a heavy conversation version of two truths and a lie?"

A hearty laugh burst out of her and she sank her teeth into the skin on his chest just enough to make him squirm. "Okay, it's official, you get me."

"The sewing machine, right? You're not going to inflict paisley on me?"

She nodded. "And I like my bedroom furniture…it would be a nice upgrade from the futon you've got in the second spare room."

"As soon as we can coordinate some days off, we'll do an official move-you-in day complete with pizza and beer."

“It’s not a lot of stuff, baby. We could handle it just you and me and your truck.” She yawned again and pressed a sweet kiss to the spot where she’d just bitten him.

“How about, I wouldn’t mind making a big deal about you officially turning this into Casa Foster-Minelli?”

She shrugged lazily, her eyes closed for good again. Her words rolled lazily against his skin. “Okay by me.”

It was okay by him, too. The perfect kind of okay.

CHAPTER EIGHTEEN

"Three weeks I've been waiting for this, hurry the fuck up."

Dani stared at Jake with more than a little amusement. "It's a single run of stuff in two trucks, and we're getting pizza for everyone afterward. We might as well let them digest their breakfast a bit now."

"There's a storm coming in later. Do you know how long it took me to get everyone with a day off? *Three—*"

"Three weeks, asshole, yeah, we heard you. Sue us for having jobs and lives and shit." Matt reached his fork across the diner table and stabbed a hash brown off of Jake's plate. Dani stifled a giggle by burying her face in Jake's shoulder. He wrapped an arm around her and from the way his muscles bunched and flexed against her cheek, she imagined he was glowering at his brother. Or as Fosters referred to it, bonding.

From the next booth over, Rafe made a big production of needing more coffee and Dean pretended to get a work call, and Dani thought her heart might just explode from the joy of it all. In their own weird manly ways, all of their brothers were showing their…well, support might be too strong of a word. Acceptance of Jake and Dani's relationship.

She'd take it.

Even her parents were being pretty cool about her moving out. Now that she was finally vacating her room, they were talking about turning the front of the house into a Bed & Breakfast—like they needed more work.

The diner door swung open and in rushed Olivia. "I'm here!"

"And you're not going to lift a single thing," her husband said just as quickly.

"Wait, what?" Dani's head jerked up. "Olivia Minelli, have you been keeping secrets from me?"

"Rafe!" Olivia stamped her foot. "Do you not remember me telling you that we shouldn't tell anyone until after twelve weeks?"

"Do you not remember *me* telling *you* that moving wasn't a job for a pregnant woman?"

"Nope. I was too busy thinking about how weird it was that my husband had been transported back to the 1960s." She smiled brightly. "Yeah, I'm knocked up. Not an invalid. Just pregnant."

Dani launched herself out of the booth, almost tripping over Matt's feet as she threw her arms around her sister-in-law. "Oh my God, I'm so excited for you guys. How are you feeling?"

"I'm fine. A little nauseous in the morning, but it's still early days. We've known for two weeks —since Rafe went back to work."

"My mom's going to be thrilled."

"Ooh, good. You can tell her." Olivia reached for Rafe's coffee cup, which he moved to his far hand. "I can have coffee!"

"And I made you a cup before you left for work this morning." He tugged her into his lap and she pressed her hands to his face, giving him a soft look.

"When are you going to stop being such a Neanderthal, hmm?"

"When our kid goes off to college?"

“Damnit, that’s not the right answer.” She kissed him, then pointed to the cup. “Now give me your coffee.”

He gave her his coffee.

Dani laughed, because she knew that these men of theirs were lovely in many ways, but they definitely had caveman tendencies. She’d thought the same thing about Jake more than once. They weren’t in any hurry to start their own family, but when they did, she was sure he’d be insufferable. In the best way, and they’d always give in when they weren’t actually in the right.

Once Olivia was re-caffeinated and had regaled everyone with stories of the first so-called celebrities getting settled in for the movie that was going to be filmed in Pine Harbour over the spring—so-called, because the only arrivals so far were the assistant director and the supporting actor, someone none of them had heard of—they loaded into their various trucks and headed for the Minelli house.

Dani had slept there the night before—the last night she'd sleep apart from Jake unless one of them had to work, she promised him—and before he'd picked her up for breakfast, she'd stacked the last of her boxes on the main floor. It was silly, doing this when they could have moved them a few at a time and already be done, but this group effort was also *normal*. And she got that Jake wanted a piece of that for them, a symbolic act. The opposite of hiding.

Her mother had baked muffins while they were out, and pressed them into Olivia's arms with a surprisingly kind smile. Maybe she'd guessed their news, or at least hoped.

The boys made quick work of the boxes, which fit into two truck beds, and Dani's few pieces of furniture from her room and the garage all fit into Matt's truck. Tom grumbled about his SUV being unnecessary, but Jake told him he needed to come along to drink their beer. “We’ve already placed the pizza order, might as well.” With a casual wave at her parents, standing on the porch, he lifted his voice. “You guys coming, too?”

“That was nice,” Dani said as Jake started his truck. “Inviting my parents over. They’ll appreciate it.”

He grinned at her, the rugged lines of his face a handsome contrast to his happy smile. “I have a vested interest in keeping them happy. I invited my dad, too.”

“Did you order enough pizza?”

“Oh yeah, don’t worry.” He squeezed her hand. “I planned for everything.”

She believed him. Jake was nothing if not a planner. Living with him was going better than she’d imagined, in part because he took care of so much. He planned a weekly food menu, did most of the shopping, and even folded laundry. The type of stuff that his brothers would tease him for, but somehow Jake made flipping through grocery flyers dead sexy. Maybe because when he glanced up and found her watching him, he'd flick them to the side and crook his finger as if to say, *Woman, in my lap, now*. And then they'd make out for a bit.

Yeah, living with Jake was good. It still gave her a thrill to pull into his drive and think *I'm home*. They hadn't talked about weddings or anything like that again in the three weeks since Valentine's Day, but there was no hurry. They'd get there, she had no doubt.

The boxes of clothes were directed upstairs, and they'd bought new bookcases to flank the fireplace in the living room for her collection of thrillers and romantic suspense novels. Her parents arrived in time to unpack the framed photos, and Dani and her mother got into a fight about the best way to arrange them on the mantle. She let it go, because it didn't matter, and then her heart skipped a beat when she noticed Jake drift through the living room and fix it back to how she wanted it once they'd moved into the kitchen.

She didn't have a lot of kitchen stuff, which was good because Jake had more than enough for both of them. But over the years her mother had given her a number of cookbooks, and she added them to Jake's collection. "Where's the box marked linens?" she hollered, and when no one answered right away, she jogged into the front hall, almost running into Jake's father. "Mr. Foster, welcome!"

"I think you can call me William," he said with a smile that look just like Jake's. "Or if you want, I'm happy to respond to Colonel."

"Stop flirting with my girl, sir," Jake said, joining them in the hall. He held out a hand for his dad to shake. "Thank you for coming."

"Well, you know how we retirees are, living on fixed incomes." He winked. "Anything for a free lunch."

"Who said it would be free? This is a working party. You can help me find the linen box and unpack it." Dani gave him a quick hug.

Jake growled, so after she took his father's coat and the Colonel headed to the kitchen, Dani wrapped her arms around the man she loved and gave him a longer, tighter squeeze.

He pressed his lips against her forehead. "Love you, gorgeous."

She gazed up at him, thinking it wasn't possible to be any happier. "Love you too."

The moment was broken with the sound of shattering glass, and Jake went to deal with that while Dani found the box she wanted in the pile at the door, but before she could get back to the kitchen, her phone rang. "Can someone answer that for me?"

Tom snagged it off the counter and waved it in the air. "It's Zander on FaceTime." He tapped the screen. "Hey bro, what's up?"

"Jake emailed me and told me to call. Something about a pizza party."

Dani slid a sideways glance at her boyfriend, who was calmly sweeping glass into an empty box. He finished up and tucked the broom away before nodding toward the phone. "Yep. Hey, man."

Zander laughed. "What's up? I usually get in shit for not being around to work. And all I'm doing over here is protecting the country."

That got him the expected round of boos and hisses from his fellow soldiers. The rivalry between the regular force and the reserves was alive and well, and bouncing noisily around Dani's kitchen.

Her kitchen. That she shared with Jake, the bestest boyfriend in the world because he'd organized a secret housewarming party for her.

"Well," Jake drawled as he turned toward her, dragging the attention of the room with him.

His words were still for Zander but his gaze was locked on her face. "I'm going to ask your sister to marry me, and I wanted to do it front of absolutely everyone in our family."

Dani heard Jake say those words like they were any other words, not crazy words, and all the blood in her head rushed to her heart. That made sense—it was beating faster than she'd have thought possible. But man, she needed *some* blood left in her head to think. And remember every moment.

"You're going to do what?" she asked stupidly, because she'd *heard* him, but she wanted him to repeat it before she passed out.

"You okay?" His eyes crinkled in delight as he crossed the kitchen and dropped to one knee right in front of her.

"You're enjoying this, aren't you?"

"Absolutely." He took her hand, kissing her knuckles before looking back up at her. "Dani Minelli, I have loved you for a very long time.

And for too long, I let stupid shit get in the way of that. I hid my desire for you, and I'm so glad you saw through me."

"In hindsight, you weren't very good at keeping that a secret," she whispered.

"I had no clue, and I'm still annoyed about that," Rafe piped up from the corner.

Jake didn't toss him a shut up or wag a middle finger in his direction. He just stared up at Dani like she was his whole world, and she got that, because he was hers.

"I know it's quick, and we can have the world's longest engagement if you want, but I'm done hiding how I feel, Dani. I want you to be my wife. I want to fill this house with babies and memories, and I want the whole world to know it."

"Okay."

He laughed and squeezed her hand. "Wait, I haven't officially asked you yet."

"I know, but I've waited a long time, too. I'm a little over-eager."

"That's good." He was rubbing her knuckles, and she was staring at their hands so hard, she didn't even notice him pull a ring from his pocket. "I understand that it's Italian tradition for a ring to be offered at an engagement party. I've wanted to give you this ring for weeks now. Thought about it on Valentine's Day. Almost pulled it out a few times over breakfast. Once when you washed all my work socks. All equally good moments. But then I thought…no, it's gotta be in front of people."

"So they can all see me cry?" she sniffed, then laughed. It didn't matter.

"So they can all see how *proud* I am to be yours. So there's no doubt this is something to be proud of, this love between us." He held up the simple gold band with a diamond solitaire sitting on top of it. "And maybe so there'd be witnesses when you say yes, because I'm going to hold you to it. Dani, will you marry me?"

She nodded, and opened her mouth to say yes, but he was already on his feet and kissing her, holding her face so gently it made her heart ache. She was used to Jake's bruising passion, his possessive holds and lusty expression. This side of him—the side that knew how to kiss in front of siblings and parents and still be utterly adoring—was a surprising treat.

Easing back from his tender kiss, Jake stared into her eyes. "Yes?"

"Yes." Another nod, and with shaking fingers she took the ring from him, sliding it onto her left hand as he stroked her arms and around to her back. "It's perfect, Jake. I love it."

"You're perfect." His voice was low and for her ears only, his gaze still glued on her face even as she stared at the ring on her finger. Every time she looked up at him, he was there. Waiting for her.

"Are you guys going to let us in on the happy celebration moment, too?" Dani peeked past Jake to see Olivia bouncing up and down, waiting for a hug. With a squeal, she pulled her sister-in-law in, and Jake stepped back, accepting handshakes and backslapping hugs from all the men. Then the parents crowded in, looking pleased, and Dani let out a sigh of relief she hadn't realized she'd been holding back.

"I thought he'd have asked you sooner," her mother murmured after they hugged. Dani shrugged. "He came to see us on Valentine's Day."

"What?"

"I tried to talk him into waiting, but I didn't think he'd do it. He's quite set on you, that boy."

"You what?" Shaking her head, Dani dragged her mother back a sentence. "Why did you try to talk him out of—"

"Daniella, it's rude to not *listen*. I didn't say talk him out of anything, just…we suggested he not be hasty." Dani followed her mother's gaze to where Jake held court with the men. "But I suppose it isn't that hasty for him."

"Or for me. Keep your fingers out of my business, Ma."

"Can't. You'll understand…" Anne sighed. "Well, you know."

"I do. No comments allowed from the peanut gallery on when/if we have kids, either."

"If?"

Dani laughed at the horrified look on her mother's face. No way was she relieving her fear, even if it was definitely *when* and not *if*. Having Jake Foster's baby…that was a definite plan. At some point.

The pizza arrived soon thereafter, and people settled around the kitchen and open dining room area with food and drink and a million questions.

Zander's FaceTime call kept dropping, so Jake opened up his laptop and called him on Skype instead. Ten minutes later, her brother disappeared, returning on screen with his own slice of pizza.

"Where'd you get that?" Rafe asked.

Zander smirked. "Duty corporal."

"Fu—" Their mother cleared her throat and Rafe ground his insult into the ground. "Fun, I mean."

"It is fun," Dani insisted, nudging her brothers out of the way to get some valuable screen time. "Hey, Zander. I took the toy box."

"That's mine, you brat."

He wasn't wrong. It had technically been his first. But then everyone else had grown up and moved out of the house, and as the last *kid* to leave, she'd taken it with her.

"You're never going to need it," Rafe piped up. "I think I should have it." And then with a smug-as-all-get-out grin, he relayed the good news about Olivia's pregnancy.

Fingers drifted across the nape of her neck and Dani twisted her head to smile at Jake. Her fiancé. A secret smile played across her lips and she let it be just for him while everyone else talked at the computer. She slipped her hand into his, and he pulled her away from the crowd. "Thank you," she whispered. "For making my entire family a part of today."

"You liked that?" He kissed her temple, then brought his lips to her ears. "Good."

The way he said it, a sexy combination of confidence and anticipation, made her wonder what else he had planned for the day. "So all these people…they're going to leave soon, right?"

"Eventually. There's a storm coming, you know." He kissed her, softly like before, but his tongue teased the seam of her lips this time. She parted for him and he tasted her for just a second. Just long enough to get her motor going.

Ha. Who was she kidding? He just needed to look at her to do that, and he'd been looking a lot today. "A storm, eh?"

"Big one. Might need to stay inside all weekend long."

"I can't wait."

"You don't need to wait any longer, gorgeous."

EPILOGUE

"Aren't they amazing, these men of ours?" Olivia tucked her head against Dani's shoulder.

"Oh, yeah." Dani stared at Jake as he carried a piece of dock into the lake. The men—Jake, Rafe, Dean, Matt, Tom, and Sean—had spent the morning sinking support pilings underwater, and they'd worn wet suits, but the late May afternoon sun was unseasonably hot, and Jake had since stripped down to a pair of board shorts.

Putting in a dock had been a most *excellent* idea. It was a bit of a hike to get to the lake—

Jake's property was a long, narrow slip of land, with a forest and a rocky descent between the house and Lake Huron. She hadn't known about the lake access until one morning a few weeks earlier when Jake woke her up at an ungodly hour with coffee and what was starting to look a lot like a girly wedding binder.

"So I've been thinking more about your dock idea for the wedding," he'd said, like that was an acceptable thing to do at quarter to six in the morning instead of *sleeping*.

"It's okay, baby, I don't care," she'd mumbled, flashing him some boob in an attempt to lure him back to bed. It didn't work. Instead he coaxed her out of bed and into a hot shower, and then made her pancakes while he talked about the forest and a tent and mowing a bigger back lawn.

"You've totally lost me," she'd said for what felt like the tenth time, but probably was the first one she'd said out loud.

"Come on."

He'd bundled her up and they'd headed back beyond the fence that she'd always assumed was the border to his property. Apparently not.

And now he had all of their brothers hard at work. Plus some of his crew. Being a builder had its perks, apparently. One of them being drool-worthy abs, and another being a lot of power tools.

The women were sitting on a large landing halfway down the newly built stairs descending to the lake from the top of the hill. The landing functioned like a deck, and Dani had carried two chaise chairs down to it in the name of comfort for her pregnant friend. That she also got to sit and ogle…well, just her fiancé, because most of the other good-looking men below were related to her.

But Jake was definitely ogle-worthy all on his own.

"You okay there?" Olivia laughed and pressed her cold bottle of lemonade against her neck.

"This is the first summer I haven't had to avert my eyes around him. I'm going to be disgusting in my appreciation for a good while yet."

"You guys pick a date yet?"

After months of dancing around the details, because nothing had felt quite right, once Jake came up with the idea of building a dock, all the rest fell into place. She even had her dress ordered.

"We're thinking last weekend in August. Just need to finalize a caterer and make sure we can get tents rented."

"If you can't rent them, I bet he'll just build them." Olivia pointed to where Jake was barking orders like a drill sergeant. Which he was. It made Dani laugh.

"Jesus, you even find his bossiness a turn on?"

Hooking a finger over her sunglasses, Dani tugged them off her head and onto the bridge of her nose. Everything Jake did was a turn on. It would be best for everyone if she had some privacy as she ate him up with her eyes.

RUNNING water and girly scents greeted Jake as he entered their bedroom. He found Dani in the bathroom, filling the rarely used tub.

"Taking a bath?" he asked drily. He didn't mind —hell, he wanted to watch—but it wasn't like she'd busted *her* very fine ass all day installing a dock.

"It's not for me, silly. Strip."

He didn't need to be asked twice. He dropped his swim trunks on the tile floor and padded across the room. She patted his butt and pointed to the water. "In you get."

Snagging her wrist, he worked his other hand under her shirt. "Join me," he muttered, kissing that spot on her neck that always got her going.

"Can't. I'm babysitting tonight, remember?"

That worked for him. "Tell me more about your dirty babysitting fantasies."

She giggled as she pulled away. "No, for real. I told you, Ryan has a…well, he wouldn't call it a date. But he's going out, and he asked me to watch the kids instead of their grandparents, so I'm assuming he doesn't want them to know that he's going out. Ergo, a date."

Jake tipped his forehead against Dani's. He did remember now. *Damn.* "Do we know who the mystery woman is?"

"Nope. Still a secret."

"What time do you need to be there?"

"An hour from now, but I wanted to—"

"Nope, that's long enough. Strip." He twirled his index finger in a circle, pleased to see she didn't bother fighting.

"You know at some point we're going to have to stop going at it like bunnies, right?"

"Not any time soon, I hope." He licked his way down her neck, already half hard and ready to be inside her. "God, you taste good. Shirt off, please."

Her whole body shook with laughter as he shoved her t-shirt up and mouthed over one of her nipples.

"What? I said please."

"Sure." She wiggled out of her shorts and climbed into the tub, holding out her hand in invitation. "You coming?"

"After you."

They made short work of getting clean, then Jake leaned back, pulling Dani backwards with him. He knew he didn't have a ton of time, so he worked efficiently, teasing all the places that got her hot and bothered without spending enough time in any one place to finish her off. He liked fingering her best, that slippery slide into her pussy the best feeling on earth as far as giving went. Her riding him beat it all, of course. But turning her on with just the touch of his fingers…that was a power trip. He could do a lot with his hands. Build houses. Fire a sniper rifle with deadly accuracy. Comfort friends in need.

But everything paled in comparison to this connection they had.

“I love you,” he said, his voice thick with emotion, and she echoed the sentiment, arching out of the sudsy water under his touch.

He couldn’t wait to make this woman his wife. He’d build a hundred docks if she wanted. She’d thought she was being stubborn and difficult over the early months of wedding planning, but Jake hadn’t cared. He loved that Dani waited until the right answer presented itself. She didn’t settle, ever, and that made the wait all the more worthwhile.

"How do you want me?" he asked with a groan as she rocked her ass against his now rock-hard cock.

"Like this." She lifted up again, tipping her hips down enough to welcome him into her body, and then they were groaning together as she stretched around him. "So good," she panted, and it really was.

At this angle, he wouldn't last long, so he resumed his teasing and stroking. The bubbles helped him slick his hands over her breasts and down her belly to her clit, then back again, but on the next pass, she clamped her hand over his as he reached her pussy. She held their fingers there and he rocked his palm back and forth over that nub of nerve endings as she touched where they were joined. Then she stroked lower, her fingertips glancing over his balls, barely able to reach as they drew tight, his orgasm coming on hard and fast. Water sloshed all around them as she swivelled her hips, taking all he had to give her and then some as she found her own pleasure against his hand and around his erection.

“Wow.”

He wasn’t sure which one of them had said it, or maybe they both did at the same time. Either way, that had definitely been *wow*. He couldn’t feel his legs and his vision was sort of spotty, but he was suddenly a big fan of bubble baths. “We should use this thing more often.”

“Mmm hmmm.” Dani slowly extracted herself from his grasp, then peered over the edge of the tub. “Or…”

He couldn’t muster enough energy to move. “Did we flood the floor?”

“Just a bit.”

“Worth it.”

“Let me guess… the builder is confident in the waterproofing membrane he laid down under these tiles?”

The builder didn't give a fuck at the moment, but as a matter of fact… "Yeah, he is."

"I'm pretty confident in his abilities, too."

"Dirty girl."

"You love it." She climbed out and pressed a kiss to his forehead. "You crashing soon?"

He might fall asleep before he got out of the tub. "Yep."

"K. I'll see you when I get home." Her voice grew distant as she disappeared into the bedroom, and he slowly followed after draining the tub. He stepped gingerly on the bath mat, then on the trail of towels Dani had tossed on the ground to sop up the water. He flipped the switch for the fan, gathered up the wet towels and lay down new ones before crawling into bed and passing out.

DANI COULDN'T STOP SMILING the whole way home. She still didn't know who the mystery woman was—Ryan had left and returned on his own. And he hadn't been gone that long, didn't smell like perfume or have any lipstick marks on his collar, or any other obvious sign that he'd been with a woman. But there'd been a softness in his face that made her heart sing. She bit back all the questions she had for him. If he wanted her to know, he'd offer the information freely.

And Ryan didn't want *anyone* to know that he was on the road to happiness again. She got that.

It still made her smile.

She parked in the garage, then walked through the house, locking up and turning off the lights. As she usually did if she was the last one up, she stopped at the fireplace and looked at the double selfie she and Jake had taken the day they'd gotten engaged.

Everyone else had left, and the snow had started falling. Outside, a blizzard raged, and inside they'd been nothing but smiles for each other. Jake had cracked open a bottle of wine while Dani documented every step of the process on her phone.

"Give me that," he'd said gruffly.

"Baby, I want to remember ever single moment," she'd protested.

He'd just given her that smile, the one that undid her every single time, and stretched his arm out in front of them at the same time as he pulled her close. "My wife," he'd whispered just before pressing the button, and the expression captured on her face made her do a secret happy dance every time she looked at the picture.

Turning off the light, she glanced back at the mantle one last time before climbing the stairs.

She crawled into bed, kissing Jake's back as he snoozed away. "My husband," she whispered, feeling blessed beyond words.

THE END

ABOUT THE AUTHOR

The author of more than thirty-five romances, and a thirteen-time USA Today bestseller, Zoe York lives in London, Ontario with her young family. She writes as both Zoe York and Ainsley Booth, and is currently chugging black coffee, wiping sticky fingers, and dreaming of heroes in and out of uniform.

www.zoeyork.com

www.ingramcontent.com/pod-product-compliance
Lightning Source LLC
Chambersburg PA
CBHW020721310726
48979CB00004B/1015

* 9 7 8 1 9 8 9 7 0 3 4 9 6 *